Jo
O'Neill

RAINBOW'S END

Hodder
Children's
Books

A division of Hachette Children's Books

Hodder Children's Books
a division of Hachette Children's Books
338 Euston Road
London NW1 3BH

Dedication

In memory of my Aunt Margaret (who emigrated to the USA when she was fifteen years old and achieved the 'American dream') with love and admiration.

Acknowledgements

I would like to thank Emily Thomas for her foresight, good advice, and the valuable time she put into this book. I appreciate it greatly.

I am indebted to Jonathan Lloyd and Camilla Goslett for their excellent agenting.

A special thanks must go to Joe and Joan O'Neill, Martin, Susan, Kate, and Andrew Davies, Johnny, Jane, Joey, JJ, and Jemma McCarthy; for their kindness, and generosity above and beyond all expectation during the wonderful holiday in Plettenburg Bay, South Africa. I am so grateful to you all for showing me this most beautiful part of the world, and I am going back!

As always I am grateful to the members of my Writer's Group: Sheila Barrett, Julie Parsons, Catherine Phil MacCarthy, Renata Aherns-Kramer, Celia McGovern, Alison Dye, for careful consideration of my work, excellent criticism, and friendship.

A very special thanks to June Flanagan for reading the manuscript at a crucial time, and giving me such great encouragement. Also, to Nikki Dempsey for her reading and saying all the right things I needed to hear at the time. And to my cousins: Joan O'Sullivan and Kathleen

O'Sullivan for continued encouragement at all times.

The biggest thanks must go to my family; John, Gerard, Jonathan, Robert, Elizabeth, and Laura for all the listening, chats, laughter, and enduring love.

And finally, Coco Chanel Axel Madsen.

'I've a right to think,' said Alice, for she was beginning to feel a little worried.

'Just as much right,' said the Duchess, 'as pigs have to fly.'

Lewis Carroll

New York – 1925

One

Through the grimy cab window I stared out at the stone towers of Brooklyn Bridge that dominated the skyline. Ahead were low-rise brownstones; below that tenements in the harbour and, in the distance, the majestic Statue of Liberty rose out of the sea.

Before I knew it I was back in the bitterly familiar streets and stores of Flatbush, Brooklyn; the dry cleaner's store with the same old faded poster showing flappers above it, the pharmacy where I used to get Bridget the housekeeper's prescriptions, and the pawnshop where I'd traded regularly on her behalf. I was filled both with excitement at the thought of seeing my sister, Alice, again, and guilty regret for having left her at the mercy of Aunt Sally and Uncle Jack. I thought of Alice's despair when I'd run away from the awful house the previous year, and wondered how she'd receive me. And then there was the fear of facing my aunt and uncle again.

Finally, the cab pulled up in front of the dull house. I got out and stood for a while staring upwards like I'd done on the very first day, my hand hesitant on the polished brass bell, scared to ring it, having no idea what kind of greeting to expect.

As soon as I pressed it a corner of the net curtain in the sitting room lifted, and there was Alice, tall and beautiful, her face a mixture of surprise and joy. There was a scrabbling sound as she wrenched open the front door.

'Ellie! I can't believe it,' she cried, her voice high-pitched with excitement as she flung her arms around me in an embrace that took my breath away. Speechless, I stepped back and stood taking her in. For the first time I was struck by her resemblance to Dad. It was in the sparkle of her eyes, the tangle of her unruly curls, her smile and the quick, sure-fired way that she said, 'Aren't you going to say something?', tears making her eyes shine like crystals.

'Oh Alice, it's so good to see you,' I finally gulped through my own tears.

'You too, I heard you'd been back home.'

'Yes, I was. I'm on my way back to Boston. I thought I'd stop by to see you.'

'How's Mam and Lucy? And baby Matthew? Is he as beautiful as they say he is?' she enquired, hardly drawing a breath.

'Mam and Lucy are both in great form. And Matthew is adorable.'

'Oh, I'd love to see him,' she said, leading the way

up the steps. The dignified way that she carried herself, her head held high, her shoulders back, was so graceful and proud, so full of possibilities. I realised how very much I'd missed my little sister.

'Who's there?' Aunt Sally came into the hall, shading her eyes from the sunlight. She'd lost weight. Her neck looked scrawny, and her cheeks were hollowed out.

'Ellie, it's you!' she exclaimed when she saw me, shrinking back like a snail in a shell, her mouth pursed in a disapproving way.

'Hello Aunt Sally . . .' My voice trailed away.

'Why didn't you let us know you were coming?'

'I thought I'd surprise Alice.'

'I really didn't expect to see you here again to be honest. You were so . . . uncomfortable when you lived here.' Grudgingly, she stood back to let me in.

'How are you keeping, Aunt Sally?' I asked, to be polite, when we were seated in the family room.

'I'm feeling poorly. My health hasn't improved one little bit since you were here, and my headaches are worse than ever. You know how your Uncle Jack is, he doesn't understand at all. In fact I'd be in bed if it wasn't for—' But the telephone rang and thankfully her rant was interrupted. She hurried away to answer it.

The door slammed, and Mary-Pat came in. Her hand flew to her mouth when she saw me. 'Ellie!' There was surprise in her voice, and a veiled, guarded look in her eyes. In a plain navy dress, a dash of lipstick on her sullen lips, her hair in heavy bangs, she'd changed into a tall, plain young lady.

Uncle Jack stepped in behind her and when he caught sight of me he looked astonished. Recovering quickly, he asked rudely, 'What are you doing here?' his mouth turning downward, his eyes sharp on me.

'I came to see Alice,' I faltered, my courage drowning in his blank stare.

So, you're on your way back from Ireland then?'

'Yes.'

Aunt Sally returned. 'Now that you're here you'd better stay the night,' she said, leaving me in no doubt that it was just the one night I'd be staying.

'Thank you, I appreciate that,' I said politely.

Alice tugged at my sleeve. 'Come on down to the kitchen to see Bridget. She'll be thrilled to see you.'

Bridget, neat in her overall, looked exactly the same as when I'd seen her last, if a little plumper.

'Ellie, it's you,' she cried, heaving herself up from her chair, holding out her arms to me.

'Oh, Bridget, it's so good to see you.'

'And you too.' Shaking her head in wonder, she said, 'My Lord! How the time's flown by. Look at you – so grown up, and so beautiful. Here, come and sit down and tell me all your news. How are things back home in Ireland?'

'Good, things are picking up after the civil war.'

4

'Thanks be to God.'

She made a pot of coffee and she and Alice both sat down to hear all my news.

Dinner was in the family room, where Bridget served shepherd's pie, while Uncle Jack ate staring straight ahead of him, looking pained from the effort of having to tolerate me.

'So, you make hats for a living I hear?' Aunt Sally asked.

'That's right, I do.'

'How enterprising, I liked the hat you were wearing when you arrived, very original. Of course I love hats, as you know. They give a sense of occasion to an event I always think.'

'Thank you.' I gaped at her. Aunt Sally had never paid me a compliment, or given me praise for anything I'd ever done before.

'Perhaps you could make me one for a concert I'll be attending at the Mansion House next month. Make a little something to match my new cocktail dress. I'll show it to you. It would be such a treat to have something unusual to wear.' She spoke with the air of a queen bestowing a favour on a servant girl.

Taken aback, I found myself saying, 'Well, of course I will, but how will I get it to you?'

'Pop it in the post. It'll arrive in plenty of time.'

'Would you like another potato, Ellie?' Alice

interrupted, seeing my amazement at Aunt Sally's nerve. We exchanged a smile.

'No thank you.'

'Things have changed since you were here. We have a girl to serve the lodgers now,' Aunt Sally said brightly.

'I still help sometimes,' Alice said defensively.

'No harm in that, except that you show no interest in what you're doing,' answered Uncle Jack sourly.

'Why should I?' Alice replied haughtily.

'Don't speak to me like that.' Uncle Jack was red-faced with temper.

Alice grimaced. Turning to me she said, 'Can you see why I hate it here?'

'Alice!' a shocked Aunt Sally cried.

Alice straightened her shoulders. 'Well, it's the truth. I do hate it here.'

Uncle Jack shot up out of his chair. 'Go to your room at once,' he commanded her, pointing to the door, like a sergeant major.

'That's fine, see if I care.' She stood up, and left without a backward glance, banging the door behind her.

Uncle Jack sat back down and picked up his fork. 'She's impossible,' he muttered, shovelling pie into his mouth.

Aunt Sally was grimfaced. Putting down her knife and fork, she said, 'Your Uncle Jack is right. Quite honestly, Eleanor, Alice is a great disappointment to us. Her school report cards are below standard, and her teachers have complained about her bad behaviour in school. She is a constant worry.'

A feeling of indignation rose up in me. 'I'm sure there's an explanation. Alice loves school, and she's always been happy there.'

Aunt Sally smiled her famous brittle smile. 'Yes, indeed she *was*. But she's changed. It started with little tantrums, which we ignored, but then when we insisted that she grow up and stop behaving so childishly she became insolent and ungrateful. Oh, it's awful. I lie awake at night wondering what can be done about her behaviour.'

'I hope she'll change back to the way she was and start appreciating all we're doing for her,' Uncle Jack added.

I kept my eyes on my plate, feeling most uncomfortable, while I fought back the desire to laugh up into his face.

'I mean what would she do without us?' he demanded of me.

'Perhaps she's unhappy? Maybe with a little encouragement . .?' I offered cautiously.

He turned to me with a taunting expression that sent a chill up my spine. 'Don't be silly,' he said.

'She's selfish,' Mary-Pat said. 'And she lolls about the house all of the time annoying everyone,' she added, to reinforce the argument.

'Perhaps if you made a little effort with her?' I suggested.

Mary-Pat laughed. 'I've given up on that.' She continued placidly eating, as if Alice was a lost cause.

It had been a shock to see how Alice's relationship with my aunt and uncle had deteriorated. And worse, she and Mary-Pat seemed to be enemies.

The tension in the room was unbearable. 'If you'll excuse me, I'd better go to her,' I said, pushing back my chair. I went from the room before either of them could raise any objection, and ran up the three flights of stairs to Alice's bedroom.

Alice was lying on her bed. I closed the door, sat down beside her, and took her hand. 'Alice, what's the matter?' Watching her staring out of the window I added, 'I think we should talk.'

She cleared her throat, turned her tear-filled eyes to me. 'I hate it here, Ellie. Remember when we first came here how awful it was?'

'Yes.'

'Well everything's like it was then, only worse; Aunt Sally's nerves are gone most of the time, and Uncle Jack is always in bad form.'

'But you and Mary-Pat became good friends. You were so close,' I said gently.

Alice shook her head. 'Not any more, she's sulky, and she's always finding fault with me.' She sat up. 'Ellie, Mary-Pat is awful. She never lets me forget that it's *her* house, though she's hardly ever around. I'm the one who helps Bridget. I run the errands, and do the wash-up, and help serve tables.' She looked at me tearfully. 'In school Mary-Pat sets the class against me.' The tears glazed her eyes. I moved closer to her. 'She's always bad-mouthing me behind my back. I try to ignore the snorts and whispers when she picks on me, but it's impossible.'

'But why is she doing this?'

Alice shook her head. 'I used to take care of her. I ironed her clothes, packed her school lunch, and even helped her with her homework. I remember one time I even stayed for detention with her.'

'How come it all changed?'

Alice glanced down at her hand in mine. 'I'm more popular with the boys in our dancing class, and everyone knows it. So to compensate she's made herself popular with the girls, and has them all on her side.' She took a deep breath. 'At lunchtime she ignores me while her friends cluster around her, talking about me. In the evenings she sneaks off to meet them, and pretends she's been with me, doing her homework. I tell her she'll be in trouble if Uncle Jack finds out. She's says it's no big deal.'

'Why don't you tell this to Aunt Sally? She always had a soft spot for you.'

Alice shook her head. 'She'd just say that I'm telling lies. She's always calling me a liar. Anyway, she doesn't take much interest in what goes on in the house. She certainly doesn't care about me. And she's neurotic about everything. She's on the phone to her friends a lot of the time, or in bed. To be honest she doesn't really want me around now that Mary-Pat and I aren't as friendly as we used to be.'

'So what do you do with yourself?'

'I spend most of my time with Bridget. I talk to her sometimes about things, and she tells me stories about her past to take my mind off the awful present. I heard Aunt Sally and Uncle Jack talking about sending me to a different school. It's for my own good they say, but I think that they feel that I'm getting in the way of Mary-Pat's progress. That's a joke because I'm cleverer than her and they know it. Anyway I don't want Mary-Pat to know how miserable she makes me.' A tear slipped down her cheeks. I brushed it away with the tip of my finger.

'How's Eamon?' I enquired tentatively. Alice all at once seemed to pull herself together.

'He's OK', she said stiffly. 'We don't see much of him now that he's at college.'

Thankful for that I put my arms around her. I could almost feel the ache of sadness in her as I held her.

'Everything's going to be OK, Alice. I'll have a word with Aunt Sally in the morning,' I comforted her.

She shook her head. 'No Ellie, don't say anything. It'll only make things worse.'

'Alice, listen, as soon as I'm on my feet in Boston I'll come and get you.'

'Oh! Ellie, I'd love to go to Boston!' she said in an awed whisper as if scared of being overheard.

'Yes, it's a beautiful city, you'll love it.'

'Oh, please, take me with you now.'

'I wish I could but you see I'm still employed and I'm not earning enough money to keep you and send you to school, and it's important that you finish school. But as soon as I set up on my own I'll come and get you.'

'Promise?'

'I promise,' I pledged.

'I'll help you in the store. I'll do anything.'

'I know you will.' I took a ten-dollar bill from my pocket book. 'Here, take this for any emergency. Keep it hidden somewhere safe. If you need me urgently, call me.'

She brightened up, now that she had some specific destination in mind and a bit of money. We sat making plans, Alice happier now that she was full of the prospect of moving to Boston in the near future.

I didn't go downstairs to say goodnight. Instead, I got sheets and a pillowcase out of the linen cupboard and made up my old bed.

We talked well into the night. She lay listening and still, taking everything in as I told her all about my holiday in Ireland, about Mam and our new baby brother, Matthew. I described our brother Ed and Maura's marvellous wedding day down to the last detail, even telling her how Johnny Sheerin, our nearest neighbour, had asked me to stay on in Ireland to be with him.

'And why didn't you stay?' Alice asked.

'Because I have a chance to make it here in America – I mean really make it, Alice, and have a big house, with servants, and a car, like we used to dream about, remember?'

'Yes.'

'And if I'd stayed in Ireland with Johnny, I'd end up like all the other Irish women we know, worked to the bone, and permanently pregnant, a brow-beaten housewife with nothing to call my own.'

'You'd be like Mam, trying to make ends meet selling jam and eggs to Nell in the shop.'

Alice then confided in me that she wanted to become a champion Irish dancer, and dance in competitions all over the world. 'See, I want to be famous too,' she said.

Next morning I left before Aunt Sally was up. Alice and Bridget bade me a tearful goodbye. 'We'll be together in no time,' I whispered to Alice as I hugged her, feeling a pang at the thought of leaving her behind.

Uncle Jack barely uttered a word as he drove me to the station.

'Thanks for the lift,' I said, hopping out quickly.

'Right,' he said as I closed the door.

I walked briskly into the station without a backward glance. Behind me, I heard his van shift gears and roar off.

As the train sped out of New York I sat staring out of the window, thinking about Alice, understanding more than anyone what a nightmare she was living through. She was just fifteen, on the cusp of adulthood, full of hopes and dreams, longing for something wonderful to happen to her, and I hadn't helped her. I wanted to go back to Brooklyn there and then to get her, but I had to return to Boston to my work. I vowed that I'd return as soon as I could, like I'd promised her, and rescue her from that horrible house.

Two

As soon as I stepped off the train at Boston South I spotted my friend Violet, whom I'd met on the ship when I'd sailed to America two years previously. I'd telephoned her to tell her I would be on the train and she'd insisted on coming to meet me at the station.

'Ellie, you're back at last,' she cried, rushing to meet me.

'It's great to be back, Violet,' I said, giving her a big hug.

Arms linked, we walked along the platform in step, Violet asking kindly after my family. I felt grateful to be back in Boston, glad of the sense of freedom this magical city had always given me.

Violet hailed a cab and we sped off to her apartment. Over coffee I talked of my reunion with Johnny Sheerin – telling Violet how he'd been my childhood sweetheart, and how he had asked me to stay on in Ireland with him.

'How romantic!' she exclaimed. 'Did you have a fling with him?'

Taken aback by the directness of her question, I wasn't sure how to respond, too shy to tell her straight out that he'd kissed me a few times. Meantime, she was scanning my face for clues to my true feelings for him. Uncertain of what they were myself, I blushed and said, 'He's a friend, that's all.' Now that I was back he seemed very far away.

After the initial gush of chatter was over I enquired about Zak, Violet's cousin and my boyfriend of a only few months' before.

'He's back home – landed himself a top job in the Bank of Boston, and he's really happy there. I'm sure you'll bump into him real soon.'

'And how's the lovely Gloria? Is she still around?' I asked wryly. Zak's childhood friend seemed a constant threat somehow.

'He sees her occasionally,' Violet said with a shrug of her shoulders. 'He says that she's good company, but I don't think that'll be enough for her. Or his parents, come to think of it. I think Gloria is part of their unrealistic expectations of him. And the fact that she's in love with him doesn't help matters.'

My heart beat faster as I asked, 'How do you know?'

'She told me so.'

'And what does Zak have to say about that?' I could hear my own voice thick with jealousy.

'He doesn't say very much but I can tell that he feels pressurised. You know I wouldn't blame him if he were to clear off one day and go round the world or something. That would be the sensible thing for him to do, if you ask me. Of course his parents would be furious. Both our sets of parents are quite alike in that way. My mother's hoping I'll find a rich Bostonian to marry. She thinks that once I find a "suitable" husband my life will be blissful, and she nags me for not putting enough effort into searching for one.'

'And what do *you* want?'

'I'd like to have more fun before I settle down.' She giggled. 'Wouldn't you?'

'Certainly, although my Aunt Mabel always encouraged me to have a career first, and then get married.'

'Very sensible of her, but it's a lot of hard work.'

'I couldn't agree more,' I said, thinking of all the effort I was going to have to put into my business. 'Speaking of which, I'd better get cracking before Dora thinks I'm not coming back.' I laughed, glancing at the wristwatch Ed and Maura had given me as a bridesmaid's present, and got to my feet. 'Thank you so much for the coffee, and for coming to meet me of course.'

'My pleasure, Ellie – it's great to have you back!' Violet smiled, seeing me to the door.

'Dora!' I called out as I flung my hall door open. When no one responded I dropped my suitcase and hurried into the workroom, where I found Dora seated at her bench, a fancy red scarf wound round her head, her dark skin glowing with good health, but her eyes scornful.

I braced myself. 'Hi Dora, how are you?'

'Fine. I was expectin' you back ages ago,' she said, glancing at the wall clock, her black mop of hair flopping over her eyes so I couldn't see the expression on her face.

'Violet insisted on coffee and a catch-up at her place. I'm sorry. How's business?' I asked, looking at the hats I'd made before I left, expecting that they'd have all been sold by now. Dora sat back and looked at me solemnly.

'Mr Samuel seems to have left us in the lurch,' she said quietly.

I pulled up a chair and sat down. 'What do you mean, Mr Samuel's left us in the lurch?'

'Oh, he goes to the selling places all over town picking up money from the previous month's sales, but there are no big sales orders; he's not pushing for more hats like before. I figure that his heart's not in the business any more. He's always rushing off to go fishing, or to see his baby son, leaving me to do everything on my own. Some of the orders I was told to rush through haven't even been delivered yet.' She lifted the hat she was making, unfurling each neat folded seam, and spreading it over the shaper carefully. 'Sometimes, I don't know why I bother, nobody else does.'

'Well, I'm back now, so I'm sure everything will get back to normal,' I said, keeping my voice steady as I met her sullen gaze.

'Yeah, well . . .' she said, unconvinced.

Looking into her scornful dark eyes, I wondered whether her complaints were justified, and if the situation was as bad as all that. Dora was a dramatic girl, the sort of person who exaggerated everything, but then I realised that she was understandably peeved at having been left to run the place for so long. I took a deep breath to stop myself from reminding her that she was being paid well for taking charge of everything, and went upstairs.

In the bedroom that we shared I noticed beautiful new lace bedspreads and pillowcases to match on our beds, and my pink and white lawn nightdress laid out carefully on mine, and knew her sullen reaction to my return was because she'd missed me.

After our lunch of crackers and cheese, I checked the order book. Dora hadn't exaggerated one bit; the orders were indeed down. I sat pondering the situation, wondering what on earth had happened between Mr Samuel, my boss, and our wholesale clients, and what was to be done. I was relying on those orders. They were what Aunt Mabel termed my 'bread and butter' hats. I was so deep in thought that I didn't notice Mr Samuel's car drawing up to the kerb outside.

'Hi, Ellie!' he called.

I went out to greet him. Dressed in a beautifully-cut suit, his hair glossed back, shoes shining, he looked immaculate.

'How lovely to see you, Ellie,' he said, giving me a

peck on the cheek. 'Did you enjoy your holiday?'

'Yes, thank you, Mr Samuel. But since I've come back I feel a little concerned. Dora tells me that the orders are down, and I'm wondering why that is?' I asked him straight out.

He looked startled at my directness for a second, and then he grinned. 'Ellie, business is always slower this time of year, with people on holiday. You know that.'

'Well . . .' The fact is I hadn't noticed a drop in sales the previous year, and then there was a limit to my knowing things before I was semi self-employed.

He walked into the workroom. I went after him. 'Mr Samuel we need to talk, I'm very anxious . . .'

He sighed impatiently. 'As I said, it's summertime, Ellie. The wholesalers are concentrating on the fall range. We should have had our hats out by now but you weren't here to design them. But don't you fret about a thing, there's the new season's batch of hats to be getting on with. I'm sure you'll come up with some wonderful ideas . . .' He looked at me encouragingly.

'I'll need some money to buy new materials.'

'Of course, I'll advance you some, OK?'

'Thanks,' I said.

As soon as he was gone, I closed my eyes and sat at the kitchen table with a cup of coffee and my ledgers, thinking about the future and what I'd need to do to improve business. From my share of the profit I was making just enough to pay the rent and scrape together money for food and all of my other outgoings. Though I needed the financial security Mr Samuel's involvement afforded me, I'd almost as little freedom as when I'd been working in the factory.

I sat restlessly, staring out of the window at the drab factory walls opposite, wondering what to do. While I appreciated the fact that Mr Samuel had been a good friend to me, taking me on, giving me a start, I now desperately wanted the freedom to experiment with my designs, to sell them independently of him. The truth of the matter was that the percentage I was receiving from him was barely paying my way.

When a letter arrived a few days later from Johnny, my childhood friend and sweetheart, I tore it open and read it eagerly.

My dear Ellie,

Since your return to America I've been thinking of you a lot. How have you been ever since, and how is your shop doing? It must have been hard for you to settle down again.

I keep thinking of you and have your photograph here beside me as I write. I envy you. Isn't that strange? To envy someone who has had to go so far away from home to make her way, when I have a home here. But then the people I love are no longer here to share it with me, and I am hurt about that.

I wish you could have stayed, but you are free to do whatever

you like, and that was all you ever wanted. Write to me again when you have a bit of free time.
Yours affectionately,
Johnny

I placed the letter back in its envelope, and put it in a drawer.

One day soon after my return the phone rang. 'Hello!' a strange voice said. 'Is that Miss O'Rourke?'

'Speaking.'

'I hope I'm not disturbing you at your work,' she continued in a sweet, breathy voice.

'No, not at all.'

'My name is Laurel Dalton. I'm telephoning to enquire if you could make me a special hat for a cocktail party at the British Embassy?'

'Just a minute, Mrs Dalton . . . That should be fine. But may I ask, how did you get my name?'

'I'm a friend of Zak Rubens. He told me about your wonderful hats. He says that you're quite the best milliner in Boston.'

'Oh! Well, how kind of him to say so.'

'I know it's short notice as the party is on Saturday evening. Do you think you could manage it by then?' There was a pause.

'I'll do my very best,' I said, trying to ignore Dora as she hovered in the background, nosey as ever.

'How about you come round for a fitting tomorrow morning?' I suggested to Laurel Dalton, giving her directions to the shop.

'Yes, I'll be there,' she said. 'Goodbye, Miss O'Rourke.'

Putting down the receiver, I turned to Dora, who was grinning widely. 'Zak recommended me, Dora!' I grinned back at her. 'That lady wants a hat for a party at the British Embassy.'

She smiled. 'You'd better make her somethin' real eye-catching.'

'I certainly shall. How kind of Zak to put in a word for me.'

'Sure was,' Dora replied, giving me a knowing look.

Laurel Dalton arrived early the next morning. A tall, striking woman, she greeted me with a warm smile and exclaimed with pleasure both at my designs, and at the samples of material I showed her.

'I'm sick of plain black,' she told me, picking out cerise velvet.

I sketched a tiny, velvet, beaded cocktail hat, which delighted her.

'Quite honestly I feel a bit nervous. Parties can be jolly awkward affairs,' she admitted.

'Just smile and the whole place will be captivated by you,' I assured her as I cut out the material, pinned it together, and shaped it on my shaper. 'I'll have it ready for you by the end of the day.'

★ ★ ★

'Oh, gracious, how lovely!' Laurel exclaimed, several hours later as she gazed into the mirror.

With her hair caught up under the hat she looked like a model from the cover of *Vogue* magazine, and the colour suited her complexion – it gave her cheeks a glow.

'I never imagined I could get a hat as pretty as this. I'll tell all my friends about you,' she enthused as she paid me cash.

When she left Dora said, 'That's one mighty pleased customer.'

'And I am one mighty pleased milliner,' I said, dancing with delight. 'With a bit of luck she'll recommend me to all her friends.'

That evening I phoned Violet to tell her about Mrs Dalton and to thank Zak for recommending me to her. 'He did me a great favour; it's given me my confidence back.'

Delighted, she promised to tell him, and invited me to go shopping with her the following Saturday morning.

Shopping with Violet was a pleasure that I always enjoyed. She always followed the latest trends, and our tastes were similar. We both favoured Parisian couture. And with her confidence, shop assistants all but bowed before her.

'Macy's first I think,' she said as we set off.

Macy's was as spellbinding as ever with its row upon row of glass cabinets, and its coiffed and perfumed sales girls. Violet strode around while I made straight for the millinery department. There I stood gazing at the gloriously dramatic hats, carried away with the latest designs by a label with *Coco Chanel* written on it. Violet too was intrigued when she joined me.

'Can I help you, honey?' an eager, smiling sales girl asked me.

'Just looking,' I said, hoping she'd move off.

'Coco Chanel is a famous Parisian milliner,' the store girl enlightened us. Turning to Violet, who was trying on one of her velvet cocktail hats, she added, 'These hats are all the rage right now. All the film stars are wearing them. We have them in several shades.'

'I'll take this one,' Violet said, winking at me behind the sales girl's back.

Afterwards, in a nearby café, I confided in her that I wanted to have a store of my very own, uptown, so I could sell more of my own hats. 'I know it'd be a big risk as there are lots of millinery stores in Boston,' I told her.

Violet was bowled over by the idea. 'They're not selling hats like yours. You could easily make ones similar to the ones we've just seen by Coco Chanel,' she said, pointing to the gold-and-white striped hatbox beside her.

'I'm not sure if I'm good enough,' I said, aware of the

wide gap between the hats I made for Mr Samuel and the exotic confections we'd just seen.

'Of course you are. You're so creative, Ellie, and you've as much brains as the next to run a business.'

'But—'

Violet tut-tutted. 'Now, don't start getting doubts. You've already proved your ability. Now you're ready to move on to the next stage.'

'Do you really think so?'

Her encouragement got me thinking. 'I'd need to attract a clientele of wealthy society women who love to shop, ladies like Mrs Dalton, and for that purpose I'd require a store close to the city centre.'

'I couldn't agree with you more. Oh Ellie, you'd make a fortune.' Violet leaned closer, and looked at me speculatively. 'Just think, you wouldn't have to rely on Mr Samuel any more. He's given you the start you needed. But you don't need him any more. He's not going to be happy about it, of course . . .' She mimicked his hangdog expression.

I got a fit of the giggles in spite of myself.

'Pull yourself together,' she snorted with laughter. 'Everyone's staring.'

I looked round to see people at nearby tables glancing in our direction and grinning at us.

'Everything is so expensive,' I said, serious once more. 'At the moment I couldn't even afford the boxes to put the hats in.'

Violet was thoughtful for a second, then she said, 'You could always approach Zak, see if he could arrange a bank loan for you. I told you, he's on the top management team with the Bank of Boston now.'

'Oh! I couldn't possibly ask Zak.'

'Why not?'

'Well, we didn't part on the best of terms, if you remember.' That was putting it mildly. Since my return to Boston I hadn't seen Zak. I had imagined running into him, and had kept a watch out for him on the street. I jumped at every call, saying, 'I'll get it' to Dora, hoping that he'd tracked me down, but it was never him. He never appeared. I hesitated. 'I haven't seen him for ages, and I certainly wouldn't like to ask any favours of him.'

'That's ridiculous! You know that Zak's a shrewd businessman; he'll only consider your proposition if it's viable, and he certainly won't let his heart overrule his head. Why don't you phone him, or better still write to him telling him of your plans.' Violet smiled. 'You know Zak thinks the world of you.'

And I knew this idea of a store had fired her up, and that she'd talk about it repeatedly until I did something about it.

'OK, I'll do that,' I said resolutely.

Violet put down her cup and stretched out her hand to take mine. 'I wish you all the luck in the world, Ellie,' she said with real sincerity.

'Thanks Violet, I don't know what I'd do without you. You're such a good friend.' And she was. I couldn't imagine a time when she hadn't been there for me since I'd known her. Everything I'd ever asked her about she'd considered carefully. It was like old times now, the two of us together, plotting and planning, like best friends in a storybook.

I was right. From that day on Violet never stopped talking about my 'new venture', as she liked to call it; whenever she popped in to see me she'd ask me if I'd contacted Zak, and when I said no I hadn't got round to it, she'd egg me on, as fervent as she'd been when the idea was first mentioned. She would discuss this new plan in low tones, in my workroom, while listening for Mr Samuel's quick footstep, or watching for his head to pop round the door. 'If only he knew what I was putting you up to!' she would say with a laugh.

Violet's belief in me spurred me on, but it was Johnny I wrote to for advice. His reply gave me the encouragement I needed.

My dear Ellie,
I hope this letter finds you as well as it leaves me. Of course you should have your own business if you have the notion to do so. You have all the talent, the guts and the ability needed to strike out on your own. I know how independent you have always been. The fact that you refused to stay here with me

proved it. And I am still sore about it. But if you're hell-bent on going it all alone I have a bit of money put by in the bank which I would be happy to give you, or loan you if you'd prefer, to help you get started.

Good luck with all your endeavours, and do keep me in the picture, even if we're thousands of miles apart. Don't work too hard or you'll go stale, and that would never do.

Your mam and all of the family are well, I'm glad to say. The weather is good for the time of year, and the cattle are thriving.

Missing you,

Johnny

I sat reading the letter over and over, thinking about Johnny's generous offer, knowing that I couldn't possibly accept it because of the way I'd deserted him.

Finally, I plucked up the courage to write to Zak at his bank, asking if I could make an appointment to see him with regard to securing a loan to start my own business. He wrote me a formal letter back arranging to meet me there at an appointed time the following week. Also, he informed me that he would see me in person, and, in order to be prepared for this meeting I was to bring a detailed business plan with me.

Three

Now that I was going to see Zak again I was filled with a sense of exhilaration. Wanting to look more adult for this meeting, I'd bought a black suit that I could ill afford. As I studied my reflection in the mirror I could see that I still had the soft face of girlhood despite my new oxblood lipstick that gave me a womanly look, and my new blouse made me seem flat-chested. But I couldn't delay any longer. Impatiently I tugged my skirt in place and, breathing in, put on my jacket. I took my handbag and keys, and stepped out into the street.

In the trolley car uptown, I felt nervous and excited all at once. Remembrances swirled thick and fast as falling leaves; on the ship gazing up at the moon, the look on his face as he held my hand.

I could still recall the pangs of pure desire that had caused my insides to lurch that first time I'd set eyes on him striding across the deck of the SS *Carolina*. I smiled to myself as I remembered how confused and shocked he'd felt when I refused to marry him and to move to

Washington. And how cross he'd been when I reminded him that I had my own dreams and they didn't include him. Certainly not after the cold reception his parents had given me. I was conscious of my own lowly origins, but nothing or no one was going to make me feel ashamed of my background or upbringing, especially not his family.

Even after we'd parted he'd continued to tug at my heartstrings.

Zak's office was in a gloomy brick building set back from the street, with wide columns on each side of the doorway.

'I have an appointment to see Mr Rubens,' I told the smart-looking girl at reception.

'Fourth floor, end of corridor,' she said with a smile.

Heart thumping, I flew up in a gilded elevator like a bird in a cage and walked down a long corridor and through glass doors. A tall, attractive woman came to meet me. 'I'm Dinah, Mr Rubens' secretary, you must be Eleanor O'Rourke.'

'Yes, I am,' I said, trying to keep the tremor out of my voice.

She checked a list on her desk. 'Mr Rubens is with a client. Would you like to take a seat? I'll let him know you're here.'

I was leafing through the latest copy of *Vogue* when the sound of the door opening made me look up to see

Zak standing there smiling, his head tilted slightly. 'Ellie, it's good to see you again.' The smile that lit up his face sent an unexpected quiver down my spine.

'Zak!' I jumped up, almost knocking an ashtray off the table. I caught my breath. In a beautifully-tailored three-piece suit he oozed confidence. My heart skipped a beat. Oh why couldn't I be like Violet, who always kept cool in these situations?

'I'm sorry to have kept you waiting,' he said, coming towards me. 'I couldn't get away any earlier . . .'

'That's OK.' We shook hands, and I followed him into his office and sat down in a chair facing him.

'You look wonderful,' he said.

'Thank you, you're looking very well yourself,' I said, feeling my cheeks burn. In the brief silence he sat gazing at me so intently that I raised my hand to check that my hat was in place.

'May I offer you a coffee?'

I straightened up. 'Well, I guess so – yes please.' I hesitated. 'If you're sure it's not too much trouble?'

'No, no,' he assured me. As he poured steaming coffee from a percolator into a white cup the expression in his eyes, his smile, the way he added just the right amount of milk and sugar, were all so familiar. Yet it was a shock to discover that, in this business environment, he was different, more sophisticated, self-confident, and aloof.

The first few minutes were awkward as we sipped our

33

coffee and smiled at each other across his leather-topped desk, piled high with papers. I couldn't think of anything to say!

'So, how was your holiday in Ireland?'

'Wonderful, thank you.'

'How is your family? Your Aunt Mabel still grooming you for fame and riches?' He grinned, and for an instant he was his old self, teasing me.

'No, I've got my own ambitions,' I said, fidgeting with my handbag.

'Ah, I see that you're nervous,' he said.

'Me? No, not a bit,' I joked, though I was shaking inside.

He leaned towards me. 'You can relax here,' he said softly. 'You don't have to keep up appearances in front of anyone. There's only us.'

I nodded and relaxed a little.

'So, you want to set up in business,' he said.

'It's like this, Zak. At the moment Mr Samuel is giving me a very small percentage of the business. I make the hats; he sells them to the wholesalers who are constantly looking for them. But I want a business of my own. It's the society women that I'm after. So, I'll need to be in the city centre to get the passing trade.' I couldn't keep the excitement out of my voice.

'Is the price right?'

'It seems to be reasonable.' I sat forward. 'I've written down everything you need to know, all the figures since

34

we started, and the projected figures for the next year.' I took a large envelope from my bag, and handed it to him. Forcing myself to speak as lightly as I could I said, 'I need a loan to buy the leasehold, and a line of credit for my suppliers. Just enough for me to start up, and I'll need to set up something legal.'

He studied the pages, ran his finger through lines here and there. As he read it I studied him surreptitiously. He was the same Zak, yet he was very much a man now, with more defined features and a stronger jawline, and full of worldly wisdom. *Stop staring*, I cautioned myself sternly as I watched him frown and widen his eyes, uneasy in his mind about something.

'Is there a problem?' I asked.

He caught my gaze. 'These figures are good. But what I want to know is can you really make a living on your own, Ellie? It'll be tough without the back-up of Mr Samuel to protect you. A milliner's job is so specialised, isn't it? I'm not sure you could earn a living just making hats.'

'Competition is a good thing, and I'd work like a demon. I can turn out the kind of hats they want. That I know for sure,' I said resolutely.

'Oh yes, I know you'd put your heart and soul into it.' He gazed at me for a moment. 'Boston is full of milliners. Every store in Boston is full of competitive people who'll be only too willing to shut you down at the least excuse,' he warned. 'The question is can you rise to the challenge? Can you make a business work in those circumstances? Stand out from the crowd?'

I stared at him. 'Yes, I can. There's nothing else I'd rather do,' I said truthfully.

He smiled broadly. 'I admire your determination, but speaking professionally, I think that you're in too much of a hurry.'

'What do you mean?'

'Ellie, you're very young, and you know very little about business. You think success is on your doorstep.' I could tell that he was seeing me as a defenceless girl, dragging myself from one job to another, whom two years of living in America hadn't wised up at all.

'Maybe not on my doorstep, but it's round the corner,' I said with confidence.

'You should take your time, relax a bit, have fun, learn to enjoy life too.'

'I'm not going into it for fun. I'm going to make my fortune,' I told him hastily. 'I have commitments.' I was thinking of Alice, and Lucy, and little Matthew, and how much I could help them if I had money.

'Admirable.' He smiled. 'I see you don't like taking advice. You're proud and stubborn, Ellie.'

'Is this what it comes down to, insulting one another?' I said, not knowing whether to hate him or to be grateful to him. One minute I thought he was the most chivalrous man on earth, the next I hated him for treating me like a child. I looked down at my hands, miserably. When I looked up he was smiling.

'Listen, Ellie, my job is about taking care of people's money. I have to get the best investments I can for them. But . . .' He took a deep breath. 'In your case, if we were to consider giving you a business loan you'd need to deposit securities with us to back you up.'

'I don't have securities, apart from the figures I've just given you, and my willingness to work hard.'

He shook his head. 'That's not enough. Someone would have to guarantee your credit, co-sign for you.'

'Mr Samuel is the only person I know who is in a position to do that, and I can hardly ask him under the circumstances.' I took the envelope from his desk, stuffed it into my handbag, Humiliated, I stood up, prepared to leave.

He came round his desk, and caught my arm. 'Don't be so hasty, Ellie. If you want to have a go at it then all right, I'll arrange the loan in both our names, and you can make me a sleeping partner.'

I looked at him doubtfully.

'I promise I won't interfere in the running of the business, and I'll help you with the financial end of things – that is, if you want me to.'

'You will?'

'Certainly, I know you, and your capabilities. And don't worry, there'll be no strings attached. I must warn you of the risks involved. There's plenty of money around at the moment, so that's not a problem right now. But things are getting tight, jobs are becoming a little more scarce.'

'None of that frightens me.'

'So I see,' he said, realising for the first time that nothing he could say was going to hold me back.

I couldn't believe what I was hearing. 'Oh Zak, I'll keep up my end of the payments.'

'I'll have the necessary papers drawn up.' He opened a drawer in his filing cabinet. Everything was arranged neatly inside of it. He found an envelope, laid it on the desk. 'I thought you might like this. I meant to give it to you before . . . before you went back to Ireland.'

I opened it. It was a photograph of me, taken by Zak in the Public Gardens, a permanent record of my first days in Boston. I was wearing the first summer dress I'd ever bought, with my hat set at a coquettish angle, a quizzical look in my eyes.

'It brings back memories,' I said.

'Yes indeed. That's why I'd prefer you to have it,' he said, his eyes thoughtful. He passed a hand over his eyes as if trying to erase some, old emotions. 'I think that will be all for now. I'll phone you when the documents are ready to sign.'

Getting to his feet he came round the desk, and laid a hand on my arm and steered me towards the door as if I was a child and he my father. Opening it with a flourish he walked part of the way down the corridor with me. I thought of the evenings we'd walked in the park holding hands. Now his hands were firmly in his trouser pockets, and there was the wide corridor between us. 'You mustn't worry, it'll all work out,' he said as we shook hands.

I left the bank in a daze, and as I boarded the streetcar I went through in my head every word of the conversation we'd had, realising for the first time the enormity of the financial time bomb we were about to set off.

The patch of blue sky outside the window of the trolley car was fading into mauve as I rode home; it calmed me. Perhaps the heartache Zak and I had been through in the past had made our reunion all the more emotional for me.

That evening I sat by my window studying the photograph. Though Zak had been delighted to see me, and had put me at my ease, there was no suggestion that he wanted to rekindle our relationship. Truthfully, he'd given no hint of it. I realised with a pang that his giving the picture back to me was a gesture of finality, a goodbye to our past.

The phone rang. 'Ellie, I was hoping you'd be still up,' Violet said. 'How did your meeting with Zak go?'

'It went very well. He's going to arrange a loan for me, Violet. Isn't that so good of him?'

'Zak's a businessman, he must have complete confidence in you.'

'I won't let him down,' I told her.

'I know you won't.'

I didn't mention the photograph.

Four

I began sending off to several top realtors for details of rental properties in the city centre. Eventually, I found what seemed to be a suitable store. Situated in the heart of the rag-trade area, the narrow street was full of elegant boutiques.

The following Saturday Violet and I went to see it. The upstairs window's tiny balcony bulged out, giving the building a crooked, dilapidated look. A straggly rose bush clung to the porch and crept up the wall, like a sentry at the gate. Inside, the hall led to a front room, a back room, a tiny kitchen that opened out to a pocket-handkerchief-sized yard – the grass rank but green.

'Oh Ellie, it's darling!' Violet exclaimed, not seeming to notice the stained walls and the grubby windowpanes – one of which was missing and covered with a piece of corrugated-iron sheeting.

Upstairs there was a bathroom and a bedroom that led to the tiny balcony off it and looked at the labyrinth of streets to the Public Gardens, a wide expanse of green, with its lines of trees in wire cages, and distant buildings.

'Fits the bill to perfection,' said Violet as we gazed up at the darkening sky overhead, listening to the whistling of the trolley cars.

'I don't know a living soul around here.'

'I still feel that it is the right place for you. With a little imagination you could make it look chic, and it isn't as if you'd be on your own, you've got strong, capable Dora to help you.'

'That's if she'll agree to the move,' I said doubtfully.

Finally, Zak phoned me to say that the loan was secured, and would I like to make an appointment to call into his office to sign the documents.

'How about tomorrow?' I asked, my voice breathless with excitement.

'My, but you're in even more of a hurry than I thought,' he said with a chuckle, but agreed to see me before closing time the next day.

The next day he greeted me all smiles but with a word of caution. 'This is a big step, Ellie.' His brown eyes searched mine, looking for doubts that weren't there.

'It's what I want,' I assured him.

Under his watchful eye, and with Dinah his secretary as witness, I read through the necessary papers. Then Zak took a shiny pen from his pocket and signed his full name, *Zachary Isaac Rubens*, in his spidery handwriting. The blood was drumming in my ears as, carefully, I wrote my full name, *Eleanor Patricia O'Rourke*, beneath his signature.

'Done!' he declared, covering the nib of his pen with a flourish. 'This is the most important day of your life, Ellie,' he said seriously. 'No going back now.' He regarded me seriously.

I met his gaze. 'No,' I said resolutely.

As soon as Dinah left his office he said, 'We must celebrate. How about dinner this evening? You don't have to get back straight away, do you?'

I looked down at my suit. 'I'm not dressed up enough for a dinner date.' It sounded like the pathetic excuse that it was, but Zak wasn't taking no for an answer.

'Nonsense, you look lovely.' He hustled me out of the door saying, 'Come on, I've booked a table at Mario's.'

Zak was all charm and consideration as we sipped our wine in the fancy restaurant off Beacon Hill. 'So, how does it feel to be a woman of property?' Zak asked, with a smile.

'A bit scary, if you really want to know,' I admitted.

'You'll be fine, Ellie, I have every confidence in you, as long you don't work too hard and burn yourself out.'

'I'll try not to.'

As the restaurant filled up, Zak talked of his banking world and the kick he got out of dealing with such ridiculous sums of money in the deals he clinched. 'Some say that this financial bubble is about to burst, but

I don't think it will happen just yet,' he remarked.

'Let's hope not,' I said, struck by how young and vulnerable he suddenly looked.

All smiles again, he said, 'Let's toast the future. Here's to all those society women who are going to look swell in your beautiful hats.'

As we touched glasses I felt a new surge of confidence, mainly because of his belief in me. Over clam chowder, followed by a delicious dish of baked cod with seaweed salad, the strain between us began to ease, and Zak enquired about my trip back home.

'It was wonderful to see them again. My baby brother, Matthew, is the most beautiful child I've ever seen, and while I was there my brother Ed got married to Maura, his long-suffering girlfriend. They're living with Mam now, and Ed is running the farm.'

'And how is your mother?'

'She's . . . well, thank you,' I said, feeling all at once a little homesick.

He touched my elbow, looked at me sympathetically as he said, 'What is it, Ellie? You can tell me.'

Although I'd vowed to myself never to tell a soul about the circumstances surrounding Dad's death, to my surprise I found myself confiding in Zak.

His eyes widened. 'What do you mean it wasn't an accident?'

In a strangled voice I heard myself say, 'Dad was murdered because he refused to join the Irregular Army at the time of the civil war,' I said bitterly.

Zak blinked as if he couldn't believe what he was hearing. His eyes grave on me, he said, 'Ellie, that's the most awful thing I've ever heard.' He took my hand, gazed at me, full of sympathy. 'I'm so sorry . . . did you find out who did it?'

I shook my head in despair. 'Apparently, the neighbours had suspected foul play but by the time someone who knew the facts was brave enough to come forward the war was over, and it was too late to bring the killer to justice.' In a shaky voice I added, 'I feel we let Dad down.' My eyes stung. There was a lump in my throat the size of a golf ball. I felt wretched as I told him how angry I'd been when I heard it. 'You see, I'd accepted that Dad had drowned, so this was like having to accept his death all over again. I couldn't understand it.'

The atmosphere was heavy with sadness and I hated myself for telling him, because it weakened me. Also, I was embarrassed by his sympathy.

Zak clasped my hands in his warm ones and said kindly, 'We don't always see things as they are, but as how they seem to be.'

'Oh . . . I shouldn't go on. I'm sorry.'

His hands still holding mine, he said, 'Talk as much as you like.'

Trembling, I shook my head. 'It won't bring him back.'

'It might help,' he said, encouragingly.

I told him about Mam, and what an awful time she'd been through. 'If it hadn't been for little Matthew I don't think she could have gone on. His birth gave her a reason to live.' Smiling I said proudly, 'He's the image of my dad.'

'That's wonderful.'

I looked at him shakily. 'I haven't spoken to anyone outside my family about this.'

'I'm glad you told me.' Candlelight cast shadows on his sympathetic face. Encouraged, I went on to tell him about my visit with Alice in New York and how unhappy she'd become living in Brooklyn. I told him how I ached to have her near me so that I could protect her from our horrible Uncle Jack and Aunt Sally.

'I don't want her to suffer any longer. I want to rescue her from that awful house but I can't afford to keep her just yet.' I told him that Alice meant the world to me and that I didn't want anything bad to happen to her.

'Don't worry too much about Alice, Ellie. She seems to be a survivor. Get yourself sorted out first then have her to stay with you as soon as you're on your feet,' Zak advised.

I guessed he was right. It seemed the sensible thing to do.

It was dark by the time we left the restaurant. We walked along in companionable silence until Zak said, 'You've gone quiet.' He glanced at me. The light from the street lamp shone on his smooth, handsome face, and shadowed his eyes. Looking at his soft, curved lips I felt a longing for him to kiss me, but then I thought of Gloria and what Violet had said about her wanting more than friendship from Zak.

'I was thinking of Gloria,' I blurted out.

Zak looked bemused. 'Gloria! What about her?'

'I heard that she's . . .' I stopped, unable to continue.

Zak looked extremely uncomfortable. 'What did you hear?'

'That she's in love with you,' I blurted out and instantly regretted this stupid blunder. I slunk along beside him, dying of shame, and hating myself for my persistence.

'Where did you hear that?'

I looked up at his flushed face and bright eyes.

'Violet told me.'

'And what would Violet know?' he demanded, irritated.

My lips felt like glue and there was a lump in my throat; I'd made a terrible mistake bringing up the subject.

'And what else did Violet say?' His angry question sounded like an accusation and an assumption that if she had said anything further it would be wrong.

'Nothing.' I was furious with myself for my tactlessness; obviously this wasn't the time to flush out my Gloria demons.

Zak's voice was loud and stiff. 'If you must know, Gloria's gone away . . . She's in England,' adding bluntly, 'not that it makes any difference, and it's of no concern to you or anyone else.'

'Sorry, I meant no harm,' I said, hoping that this would be the end of it.

He smiled, but his mood had changed. 'No harm done; as I said to you already, things aren't always as they seem, and Violet's judgement isn't always sound, no more than yours is.'

'I'm sorry,' I repeated, not knowing what else to say.

He stopped and said, with a resigned sigh, 'Why must we row tonight of all nights when we're meant to be celebrating?'

He made me feel like a child and something in me resented that. My mouth wobbled as I said, 'I don't know, or why I should even care. It's nothing to do with me.'

'That's true, and Ellie, you're an entrancing young woman. Soon you'll have all the eligible young men in Boston falling in love with you, and you won't give a fig about Gloria or me or what we do.'

It was on the tip of my tongue to contradict him, but I didn't.

When we got to my place he dropped me off and said, 'It's getting late. We both have work tomorrow.'

I longed to apologise to him and tell him that I was still in love with him, but even I realised that this was not the time or the place. He was not in the mood to be told.

'Thanks for a great evening,' I said. 'Sorry I spoiled it.'

'Don't worry about it,' he said. But the dignified way with which he said goodbye was like a reproach.

I collapsed into bed feeling sick and empty inside. What a clumsy fool I'd been, putting my foot in it like that. What business of mine was it if he was seeing Gloria again? I was the one who'd let him go. Worse still, I was anxious about breaking Violet's confidence, and involving her.

Next time I saw Violet I was determined to come clean. 'I said something stupid to Zak; I think I've caused a bit of trouble.'

'What happened?' she said, perplexed.

I told her. 'Oh, Violet, I shouldn't have said it. I feel so dreadful, spoiling everything; after all he did for me, and just as we were getting on so well together. Now it's gone horribly wrong. What must he think?' My face burned just thinking about it. 'I hate myself for hurting him so,' I cried.

Violet cut me short with her laughter. 'Ellie, you're so dramatic. You probably shouldn't have mentioned Gloria, but then, in another way, perhaps it was the right thing to do. At least he now knows that she's still coming between you both, which is silly.'

'That's the thing,' I sniffed. 'I don't know if it is silly.'

'What do you mean?'

'I get the impression that Zak is keeping something to himself.'

'What gives you that idea? What has he said?'

'It's more what he didn't say.'

'Don't be silly, Zak is incapable of keeping secrets.'

'Oh, Violet, why does everything have to be so complicated? Why can't things be normal?'

'What's complicated, Ellie? It won't hurt Zak to do a bit of soul searching,' Violet said. 'Anyway, you and he will have plenty of time to sort things out. It's not as if either of you is leaving town.'

Suddenly, I was sobbing. 'I didn't mean to say anything.'

'You got it off your chest. Perhaps you needed to do that.'

'I wanted Zak to take notice of me. Pathetic, isn't it?'

Violet smiled. 'What's wrong with that?'

'Nothing, I suppose. But I made such a fool of myself. I don't know what to do.'

'Do nothing for the present. Make your hats, but don't wear yourself out slaving away night after night like you did before.'

'Thanks, Violet,' I sniffed, grateful that she still considered me her friend though I'd broken a confidence. I thought how different she was from me, how much more calm and serene, and I wished I could be like her. She was a true friend, and I loved her for her tactfulness.

'Oh Violet, I didn't realise how much I missed him. It was of him that I thought as I trudged those wretched streets looking for a place of my own. And here I finally thought I'd found somewhere that would make me good enough, respectable. Now it looks as if we'll never be back together.'

I felt lonely. Zak had no interest in me except as a friend and though Shirlee, my old friend and Mr Samuel's wife, had invited me to dinner, she was always so busy in her role of wife and mother. I couldn't go anyway, not until I'd sorted out my position with Mr Samuel. I wanted to let him down gently because of our friendship.

Five

'I've got the loan,' I said, waving the envelope at Dora when I got home. 'Our future's sealed.'

She took a swipe at the air with glee. 'Praise the Lord,' she said. 'No regrets?'

'None,' I assured her with a gaiety I didn't feel.

I was worried about uprooting Dora from her old neighbourhood but she reassured me that she was dying to move. 'I make friends easily, and I can't have you going to a strange place all on your own, now can I?'

'Thanks, Dora,' I said, a little happier. At least I wouldn't have to face the move on my own.

All I had to do now was tell Mr Samuel, and I was dreading it.

When he called in to tell me that the orders for my autumn range were low, adding, 'I guess we'll just have to find more ways of selling the hats,' I seized the opportunity I'd been waiting for.

'I'd like to have a chat with you about that,' I said.

'Not right now, Ellie, I'm running late for an appointment.' He removed his fob watch from his jacket pocket and glancing at it said, 'Say, how about next week, when I've got more time.' He turned suddenly, and looked at me with raised eyebrows. 'You wouldn't think of quitting now, would you?'

'No, I'm not going to leave the trade.' Hardly daring to look at him, and making an enormous effort to be tactful, I circled around the delicate subject, explaining my need to expand my range. 'I'm tired of the same old orders, Mr Samuel. I want to make hats in bright colours and bold lines; unusual hats that women will want to show off. That's why I'd like to start up on my own.'

'Huh?' He looked at me thunderstruck. 'You've got to be joking?'

'No, I'm serious.'

'Listen, Ellie, we've a good little business going here. The customers are only just getting to know your designs.' He lit a cigar, blew the smoke upwards. 'Give things a little time and new orders will come flying in. I was only saying to Shirlee last night, "Those cloches of Ellie's are the tops in quality and high fashion".'

'Thank you very much,' I managed, feeling a moment of flattery, which was instantly replaced by horror at the thought of churning out the same type of hat in large quantities for years to come.

'So, no more talk of leaving, it's a terrible idea.' He gave me a wicked smile.

'I appreciate what you're saying, but I'm after the rich clients, the women who shop at the big fashion stores.'

There was a short silence while he absorbed this. 'This isn't the proper time, Ellie – it's the height of the summer. And you're just back from your holidays and broke.'

'It's the right time for me, because I'm bored. I'd enjoy starting over on my own, putting things together, building up my very own business without leaning on you for security. It makes me feel ... stuck ... in wholesale. So, I'm going ahead with it, Mr Samuel. I've arranged a loan, and I've found a little store to rent near the city centre.' I rushed on before he could interrupt me.

Astonished, he said, 'But won't that be outrageously expensive?' I could almost see his mind trying to figure out exactly how I was going to manage this.

'It's a pretty rundown store.'

He shot me a fierce look, then recovering his composure said, 'This is madness. There's no logic to it. I won't be there to keep an eye on you and you won't manage on your own. Don't you realise that I take the worry from you, make life easier?'

'Yes, and I'm very grateful to you for all you have done for me, but I need a new challenge.'

'That's crazy talk. I thought you were nice and settled with me?'

'I don't like being settled, Mr Samuel. I'd enjoy starting over on my own, putting things together, building up my own business.'

He removed his cigar to roar with laughter as if what I'd been saying was a joke. 'You know, I can see now that I shouldn't worry about you. For such a young girl you've got plenty of nerve.' He smiled at me with new respect as he got to his feet. Taking out his watch, he said, 'Tell you what, come to lunch on Sunday, talk it over with Shirlee. See what she thinks. She's dying for you to see our new home.'

I hardly slept the night before, anxious about Shirlee – worried if she'd feel hurt by my decision, too.

Their house was a charming old brownstone in Park Drive.

'Ellie! It's so good to see you,' cried Shirlee when she opened the front door.

Pregnant again, she was clad in a silk rose frock, and with her flaxen hair held back tightly with tortoiseshell combs she looked very stylish, despite a slightly protruding bump.

'You look wonderful, Shirlee.' We were hugging one another, laughing, happy to see one another again.

'Sam's hoping for a brother for David, though I'd like a baby girl,' she said, gleefully patting her stomach.

'Congratulations! Mr Samuel never mentioned that you were expecting a baby.'

'He says it's not lucky to tell people too early, but, heck, it's there for all the world to see now.' She grinned. 'Come on in and see our new place.'

Proudly, she showed me round the beautifully-appointed lounge filled with dark oak furniture, crystal chandeliers, velvet button-backed sofas, paintings, lamps, and Persian rugs. Their wedding portrait was prominent over the fireplace; Shirlee, a fresh-faced girl in a straight, blue frock, her hair swept upward to accentuate her pretty face, Mr Samuel looking sombre in a dark suit with a white high-collared shirt and cuffs to match.

'I remember that blue dress.'

She laughed. 'My favourite colour, though Sammy won't let me use it for furnishings. He says it makes him feel cold.'

We sat down on the sofa. Shirlee, her old self, chatted about David, her son, and her staff problems. Then looking directly at her I said, 'Shirlee, I'm really sorry to be parting company with Mr Samuel but this is something I have to do.' I looked at her apologetically.

She smiled. 'I understand, you must follow your heart.'

'Mr Samuel's not too pleased.'

'Not right now, but he'll come round. The problem with Sammy is that he doesn't know what's important and what isn't to a body. I know how hard it is to make a choice like that.'

The front door banged. Shirlee placed her finger to her lips signalling me to be quiet.

Mr Samuel came into the room dressed casually in a canary-yellow shirt and plus fours. Polite as ever he said, 'Hi Ellie, glad you could make it.'

Jewel, the nursemaid, came into the room hand in hand with David, their son, a beautiful little boy, with white-blond hair and cornflower-blue eyes like Shirlee's.

He raised his arms expectantly.

'Hi, my precious baby.' Shirlee chuckled as she picked him up. 'This is my pal, Ellie, come to visit!'

'Hi David,' I began but he plumped out his lower lip and began to bawl.

Mr Samuel took him and listened patiently to his childish prattle with an indulgent smile on his face, then returned him to Jewel, who was waiting to take him for his nap.

'I'm starved,' Shirlee said. 'And lunch is ready.'

She served roast chicken, giving Mr Samuel and me the golden, succulent breast, taking only the darker meat for herself. During the meal she was like a lady-in-waiting, fussing over him with vegetables and sauces. As soon as we were served she said to him, to my surprise, 'Sammy, you're not sore at Ellie, are you? You know she's got to do this.'

'No, honey, I'm not sore exactly,' he said, giving in, and agreeing that it was the right thing for me to leave, though he didn't pretend to understand it.

As soon as the meal was over he said goodbye to both of us, and went off to play golf. Shirlee and I sat out in the garden on the swing and watched David, refreshed from his nap, drive around in circles in his toy car.

'We need to have a good talk about you starting up on your own, Ellie. You'll have to do everything properly,' she advised, going through the whole thing, the store, the furnishings.

She listened to the detail of my plans, and demanded to see the new premises before I signed for it. I told her about my partnership with Zak. 'He's the one that'll be doing the figures.'

She smiled and said that with his aptitude for business, and my creative flair, we'd make a good team.

Then she said she'd arranged to have tea with her mother-in-law. 'The old dear's a stickler for timekeeping,' she said, checking her watch.

I felt sad saying goodbye to Shirlee, fearful that I might not have her friendship for much longer.

The following week Shirlee came to inspect the store and dragged Mr Samuel along to make sure it was suitable. While she clucked like a mother hen, asking relevant questions and giving her opinion about décor and display, Mr Samuel skulked around, hands deep in his pockets, pretending not to be interested. When he suggested that I might want to knock down the dividing wall to give the store more space, Shirlee levelled him with a look and said, 'No, Sammy, Ellie'll want to have the client out back for fittings.'

When they were leaving he said, 'Here, you might need this,' taking an envelope from his inside jacket pocket. It was a typed list of names of the buyers of all the big stores, some crossed out, others scrawled in.

'Oh! Thank you, Mr Samuel,' I said with heartfelt gratitude.

'You're welcome. I was getting tired of the hat business.' His face broke into a smile. 'I have my eye on a new market.'

'What's that?' Shirlee eyed him with curiosity.

Mr Samuel livened up. 'I'm thinking of manufacturing clothes for sporting activities such as golfing and fishing, that sort of thing.' Taking a cigar from his breast pocket, he lit it and said, 'It's the thing to be getting into right now.'

'You mean you're giving up the shirt makin'?' asked an astonished Shirlee.

'I'll continue with them. I've got plenty of space in the factory, and I'll hire more staff.'

I was shocked at his quicksilver mind, or maybe this was something he'd been planning all along. He certainly wasn't one to waste an opportunity. Shirlee was even more impressed.

'Gee, honey, that sounds just the thing to be lookin' into. Right up your alley.' She nodded approvingly.

'After all, who knows more about golf and fishin' than you do?'

'Absolutely so.' He flashed me an arrogant smile as he led her out of the store.

Six

We moved on a scorching hot day in August in Dora's brother Chuck's van, which was the cheapest mode of transport we could find. Chuck brought his friend Billy along to help with the lifting.

As we rattled off to the city centre I sat tense, asking myself if I had done the right thing, knowing that as soon as I was alone all my previous doubts would come rushing back.

'Here we are,' I called out when we arrived at our small street behind the row of posh stores on Charles Street.

'This!' cried Dora, easing herself out of the van and straightening up to gaze disdainfully at our new home, while I took the keys from my pocket, opened the door ceremoniously, and proudly stepped inside. It smelled of mildew from being shuttered up for so long.

'Phew, it's worse than I thought,' Dora declared, waving her hand in front of her nose.

'A lick of paint and a bit of fixin' here and there will do wonders to it,' Chuck assured her, sweeping through the hall and into the front room, flinging open the window shades and stirring the dusty, hot air.

'The bedroom is big enough for us to share, so you won't have to sleep downstairs,' I said, to humour her. 'And look, here's a wicker chair we can put in the porch for a waiting client,' I said to try and encourage her.

'That's if we ever have any,' she said, gazing around her.

Chuck and Billy started bringing in our things from the truck; bales of material, design books and magazines, boxes marked *Threads*, hold–alls bursting with clippings, boxes of photos, wrapping paper. Chuck staggered in, carrying a steel filing cabinet stuffed with copies of all our personal correspondence and lists of clients.

The furniture was sparse; two beds, and mattresses, two kitchen chairs, an old scrubbed table, a sagging sofa and an easy chair donated by Shirlee, and my dressing-table and a collection of plates that I unpacked.

While I stacked the cutlery, saucepans and a skillet in the kitchen drawers and on shelves, Dora put the broom and mop and dustpan and brush in the cupboard under the stairs, cheering up, humming a ragtime tune; then together we carried the bulging pillow slip filled with our clean bedding upstairs, to make the beds up.

By evening we'd unpacked enough cardboard boxes for us to get settled in, and left the unopened ones until we'd painted the rooms first. Then while Chuck and

Billy tidied up, Dora and I went down to the deli on the corner to buy a cooked meal for supper.

When we returned, Chuck and Billy were seated on chairs in the cool kitchen, hands washed clean and waiting to be served. We put the bowls of piping hot meatballs in tomato sauce and boiled rice in the centre of the table, together with the salad of cucumber and beetroot, and thick white bread.

'Eat up, now don't be shy,' Dora told them as she shovelled a mountain of food on to each plate while I cut slabs of bread and spread them with butter.

'This is real good,' Chuck said appreciatively.

Billy nodded, helping himself to seconds.

'The least I could do,' I told them, handing them each a bottle of root beer.

Afterwards Chuck leaned back and placed his hands on his stomach contentedly. 'You'll need to be a jack of all trades to get this place right, Ellie. There's plenty of fixin' up to be done,' he warned.

'Don't I know it?' I sighed, gazing around the room.

'If you want help with the decorating I'll be happy to oblige. Don't forget there are the safety inspectors. They'll have you plagued if you don't keep the place right.'

'That'd be great, Chuck, but I can't pay you much!'

'You can make up for it when you make your first million.'

'It's a deal! Thank you,' I agreed.

★ ★ ★

After they'd left, I had a long soak in the tub. In our bedroom I unwrapped the framed photograph of Mam and Dad from its layers of tissue paper, and placed it on the little mantelpiece over the boarded-up fireplace. I gazed at Dad, in a collar and tie, his face clear and dignified, standing proudly behind Mam, in her best black dress and shawl. Beside it I placed a photograph of a smiling Aunt Mabel wearing a wide-brimmed hat bedecked with a garland of flowers.

While Dora sat on the edge of her bed, braiding her hair, I stretched out on my bed and smiled up at their faded faces, hoping that they'd be proud of me if they could see me now, settled in my own place.

I fell asleep and dreamed that I was sitting on the riverbank with Mam and Dad, Alice and Lucy, having a picnic, and listening to the murmur of the river. I woke up sorrowful, anxious about Alice, wishing that she was here with me, and tears trickled down my face.

'Ellie? Are you all right?' Dora called softly.

'I was dreaming about Alice. I'm worried about her, Dora.'

'Well, write to her. Ask her how she's doin'?' she said gently. 'But try and get some sleep for now.'

I woke up late. The bedroom was bright, the curtains open. Downstairs, Dora, in a housecoat, was perched on a creaking ladder painting the workroom, her hair concealed in an old turban.

'Why didn't you call me?'

'You needed your beauty sleep, an' I wanted a bit of peace and quiet to get started. This is our first day in the city, hall-el-u-iah!' she sang as she slapped the dove-grey paint on the walls.

Chuck arrived soon afterwards and, after a cup of coffee, he began painting the front room. The cable man came to install the telephone, and I started on an endless round of chores waiting to be done. But to me all the jobs were enjoyable because I felt that I was getting somewhere.

At lunchtime the two of us took our sandwiches to the park to get away from the overpowering smell of paint. It was seething with people; the men were in shirtsleeves, the women in pretty print frocks. We sat in a clearing, shaded by trees from tall brick houses and the fleet of shiny black cars that lined the road. There, in a pool of dappled light, we ate our Bologna sandwiches, listening to the hum of traffic and the cries of over-excited children racing around or wrestling one another. A happy-looking couple linking arms passed us by, reminding me of Zak and me walking in this very place when I'd first come to Boston, and I felt sad that our relationship wasn't like that any more.

In the afternoon I went to a fabric wholesaler to buy

damask curtains for the front window, and cushions to liven up the couch. As soon as the paint was dry, Dora and I took great care to drape the curtains evenly on the windows to give a good first impression.

After supper, drowsy with the heat, I sat in the yard making a list of materials and trimmings I would need to make my hats.

Next day we set off to the supply store while Chuck painted the word *Chapeau* over the door in gold. Each letter shone in the sunshine. Apart from the usual requirements, I purchased a length of flowered cotton and one of fine lawn with eyelet holes to make jazzy sun hats. Dora clicked her tongue disapprovingly, and pointed out that it was the height of the season and most women would already have sun hats as it was properly summer.

'Not ones like the ones I'm going to make,' I told her.

'So you're hopin',' she said, not at all convinced.

Back in the workshop I cut out a variety of hats; straw boaters with brims, plain white floppy sun hats. Dora didn't say a word, just ran them up on the sewing machine. Together we toiled, stringing beads for trims, adding a bunch of fake cherries to a summer cloche. We worked late into the night, fiercely anxious to open up as soon as possible.

We continued like that each day. Often Dora made her own brand of trim, gathering garlands of flowers together into a perfect bright bunch for a side trim, or placing a big flower on the side of a sun hat, her head bent low, her skirts spread wide around her, her needle clutched in her hand. The stolid way she worked gave me confidence, but often, at the end of a long day we'd argue pointlessly over a design or a colour. I'd start to remind her that it was my store, only to be silenced by her quick tongue. Then I'd remove myself, make a cup of coffee to calm down, only to return to find her eyes soft, and her smile warm as ever.

At the end of the first week we displayed the hats in the window, and put a *SUMMER SALE* sign up above them. During the morning there was a steady trickle of young girls from nearby offices, hoping for a bargain.

Each day was different. Sometimes, a woman with a bag of groceries would pop in to try on a hat, or a young lady passing our store window with a dog might stop by to have a browse, then come in to try on a hat, while Dora, eyes anxious, held the dog lead. Sometimes, a customer would just pick out the trim.

At first Dora was shy with the customers. She would raise her eyebrows quirkily as she studied them, but say little. As she warmed to them, she became more confident and would voice her opinion.

Soon she became the darling of the clients; they liked chatting to her, and she had the knack of giving each one the impression that she had all the time in the world for her alone.

Gradually we settled in and the clientele changed. Society women who frequented the top fashion houses started coming to us. Some of them, bewildered by choice, asked our opinion. We were patient with them, making sure they liked our suggestions and didn't think that we were taking liberties with their own taste. This took up much of our precious sewing time – so much so that we were working at full speed until midnight.

Zak phoned one evening as I was clearing up the store, to enquire as to how I was getting on.

'Things were slow at first, but we're getting busy now, and I'm chasing orders.'

'I'm glad to hear it. Being your own boss isn't easy. Do you want me to stop by and look at the books?'

'No thanks, I'm managing fine for the moment,' I said, not sure why I was putting him off.

The days zoomed by. As our sales increased we became more daring in our styles. There was a dash to every hat, something individual or quirky about each one of them. Out shopping, we'd doll ourselves up in our latest creations. There was nothing hesitant about us. We were two young women who looked as if they knew exactly what they were doing, even if that wasn't the case at all. People turned to stare after us.

Money was tight for those first couple of months.

Worried about the expense of everything, I juggled my time between making hats and attending sales meetings in the hope of finding new outlets prepared to stock them.

There was little time to cook a meal, and often we'd forget to eat at lunchtime. In the evenings when I wasn't making hats, I'd sit at the kitchen table dealing with bills and receipts, summarising the week's business into ledgers, checking statements. Often I'd trawl through the phone book searching for outlets that might be prepared to stock my hats. Then, I would fill the bathtub and soak in it for ages, wondering if I was doing things properly, and whether I should seek out Zak's opinion on my progress.

Violet remained kind and supportive. She had the true fashion follower's flair for detail, and was full of praise and encouragement though she rarely gave her opinion without my asking it. Also she made sure we ate properly by bringing mouthwatering slices of quiche or chicken pie from the deli. Occasionally, she cooked supper at her apartment and invited us over. She would have girlfriends or colleagues round expressly to introduce us and tell them about our hats.

But it was the invitation by post to a housewarming party at Zak's new apartment that took me completely by surprise.

'You will come, won't you?' Violet asked, shading her eyes from the glare of the light as we emerged from the cinema, having laughed ourselves sick at Buster Keaton in *Night Shift*.

'I'm not so sure I'd fit in with his socialite friends, and besides I haven't seen him lately.'

'Oh, I wouldn't worry about that, you're likely to meet potential customers among them.'

'I must admit I'd love to see Zak's new apartment.' What I really meant was that I'd love to see Zak again.

'Go on then, say you'll come. Zak's parties can be very good fun, once the stuffed shirts have a few drinks in them.' Her enthusiasm was infectious.

'OK, I'll come. Hang on, will Gloria be there?' I asked with an abruptness that was nothing short of bad mannered.

'I'm not sure, and what does it matter if she is?' Looking me in the eye she said, 'I'd never have taken you for a coward, Ellie.'

'I'm not one,' I protested.

'Well then, do me a favour and come.' Violet was suddenly serious. 'I have the job of helping Zak to host it, and I could do with your support.'

It was the first time Violet had ever really asked anything of me.

'In that case I'll be glad to help out,' I said without hesitation.

'Good. It'll be fun.'

My doubts disappeared, and I got quite excited at the prospect of seeing Zak again.

I ran up a plain blue silk frock with matching bandeau, and recklessly bought a beautiful new pair of high-heeled shoes to match that I couldn't afford.

Seven

On the evening of the party we closed the store early. Dora went home to visit her family while I got myself ready – dabbed a final touch of powder on my nose, added a touch of extra rouge to my cheeks, fretting that I wouldn't look my best, wondering how his friends would be. What if I could find nothing to talk to anyone about?

The front door of Zak's apartment, a charming old brownstone, was paned with coloured glass. As I lifted the knocker a maid came swishing to the door. Violet at her heels, clearly expecting me, and looking lovely in a pale pink frock and a single rose in her hair.

'Ellie, I'm so glad you made it!'

'I'm so nervous,' I said in a wobbly voice.

'Don't be. You look gorgeous, and I love your dress,' she said, giving me a confidence I badly needed.

'What a lovely place!' I exclaimed at the beautifully appointed black-and-white marbled hall, and winding staircase.

'Isn't it just wonderful!' She led me to the lift, pressed a button, and we shot up to the penthouse suite, and before I could draw breath she'd ushered me to a sumptuous lounge full of glittering girls and glamorous men.

'I'll get you a tray of drinks to pass around,' she said over the loud chatter.

'Don't leave me.' I tugged the bow of her frock like a pathetic child.

'Stay right there; keep smiling as though you're enjoying yourself. I won't be a minute.' She sounded like a big sister.

I suddenly saw Zak in a group of people and caught my breath for a moment. I couldn't help staring at him, looking so handsome as he delighted his eager audience with some witty anecdote. Forgetting myself, I burst out laughing as he whirled around, almost knocking over a tray of non-alcoholic fruit cocktails Violet was carrying.

'Ellie!'

He excused himself, and came over.

'Hi, Zak.'

'You're looking swell,' he said. 'How're you doing?'

'Fine thanks.' I looked around as casually as I could.

'I'm glad you've taken the time to come to the party. Violet told me you were coming.' His smile dimpled his cheeks and I grew weak at the knees.

'Beautiful place you've got here,' I managed to say.

'Thanks. Come and meet my guests first, some of

whom could be very good for business.'

I followed him to a group of sophisticated girls smoking cigarettes in long thin holders, who stopped in the middle of their conversations to greet me pleasantly as Zak introduced me.

'Ellie makes amazing hats; she's opened her own hat store. You might like to pop in and see for yourselves.'

'Give us the address later and we'll pop by sometime,' one of the girls said.

Zak smiled. 'See, you can enjoy yourself while you're doing business. You don't have to put in all the hours in the store.'

'So I see.' I smiled at Violet, who handed me a cocktail. I raised it to Zak. 'To your new apartment, Zak, I hope you'll be very happy here.'

'Cheers,' Zak said, and we touched glasses. 'You haven't seen it properly, come on, let me show you around.' He led the way to a large green-and-white, airy kitchen.

'This is a dream kitchen,' I exclaimed, examining the perfectly fitted appliances, and the long breakfast counter with two chairs side by side.

'I don't use it much,' said Zak. 'You know I'm not much of a cook. Do you remember how I kept burning the toast that time we were in Hyannis Port?'

I began to laugh. 'How could I forget! But you did grill great steaks.'

He looked reflective as he said, 'We had the best time

there, Ellie. It was such fun, and I had you all to myself. In fact I felt cheated when you left.'

'I had to go, Zak.' How could he have forgotten my circumstances at that time? Uncle Jack was after me, and Mr Samuel's job offer was my ticket to freedom. That's why I'd headed for Boston – and I'd never looked back though there was no point in going over old ground now.

'I must go and talk to Violet,' I said after a pause.

'Come, let me show you round the other rooms first.'

Off the hall there was a room with beige walls, a navy-wing chair and leather-topped desk. 'This is where I spend most of my time. See, through that window – there's Fenway Park over there where the Boston Red Sox baseball team play their home games. And the Charles River is just a short walk away.'

'Perfect location,' I said, going to the window to look out at the familiar landmarks. That's when I noticed three photographs in silver frames on the wall and froze. There was one of Zak and Gloria, flanked on either side by his hard-faced parents; one of Zak with a group of friends on a yacht, Gloria in the centre. The third one was of Zak with a smiling group of friends sitting on the stoop at the summerhouse in Hyannis Port, a beaming Gloria among them.

Noticing my reaction he said, 'What's up?'

'I feel like an intruder here,' I said, my eyes on Gloria's scheming face.

78

'Why should you?' he said softly.

I didn't know what to say. Embarrassed, I raised my eyes to his.

'You think Gloria and I are together? Nonsense!' He gave a short bark of a laugh at the very idea. I thought of the distrust that must have been clear in my expression as he turned away, leaving me floundering.

'I'd better go find Violet now.'

'Wait!' His voice was brusque. 'This whole stupid thing with Gloria is a mess that we should clear up right now, Ellie.' He pushed back his hair. 'It's only right she should be in those photographs. I think of her as one of the family. Growing up with my stodgy parents wasn't easy. If it hadn't been for Gloria I'd have been desperately lonely. She helped me a lot when we were kids, and she was fun, and she always included me in whatever she was doing with her friends. I couldn't have had a better childhood friend. How many girls would bother with a shy boy like me?'

Quite a few, I thought, but the reserved look he gave me stopped me saying anything. I felt bewildered at the thought that Zak enjoyed spending so much time with someone as awful as Gloria.

'You shouldn't be jealous of her.' His dark eyes were smudged against the light, making his expression unclear, but his voice sounded weary.

'I'm not,' I lied, anxious for this conversation to be over, and desperate to redeem myself.

His eyes searched my face as if he were wondering whether to believe me or not.

'I'm sorry if I upset you.'

'You haven't upset me. I'd just like you to get those silly ideas out of your head,' he said with a look that made me feel foolish. There was an awkward pause.

Suddenly inspired, I tilted my head towards the window. 'Look at that sunset. Isn't it wonderful?'

'Yes, isn't it?' He touched my elbow to steer me towards the window, where the setting sun had dimmed to an orange glow against the dark silhouettes of buildings.

The room was filled with a hazy light that blurred Zak's face, but his wonderful familiar smell of lemon soap engulfed me. I backed away, scared I'd do something stupid like kiss him.

'Zak!' It was Violet at the door. 'Ah! There you are . . .' she said, smiling at me.

'We'd better get back to the party . . .' I blushed.

'Yes.'

Violet shot us an amused glance. 'Sorry to interrupt, but I was wondering – the band's here.'

'Ah! The band,' Zak said, absent-mindedly. 'I'd better go and greet them.'

'You two looked quite serious,' Violet giggled, shooting me a meaningful look.

'Not especially – just chatting.'

The band struck up the first notes of 'Saint Louis

Blues' and the whole room burst into dancing. Everyone was up, all colliding with one another. Zak lurched towards me, and we danced in blissful harmony for a few minutes. I closed my eyes for his kiss, but when I opened them it wasn't Zak who was in front of me but a fat, balding man I'd never seen before in my life.

The food was served at midnight and afterwards we danced to 'Yes Sir, That's My Baby' and 'Sweet Georgia Brown', changing partners, but I didn't have the opportunity to dance with Zak again.

'Do you want to go?' Violet asked after we'd cleared up.

There was no reason to stay. As we slipped away I glanced over my shoulder at Zak, who at this stage was playing the perfect host by dancing, in turn, with each pretty girl there. I realised how silly I'd been to think it would have been otherwise.

Eight

The phone rang. Shirlee's muffled voice was barely recognisable. 'Ellie, there was a fire at the factory last night.'

'Oh no! Was anyone hurt?'

'No, it happened in the night, about 2 a.m.'

'Thank God for that.'

'Sammy's not here. I'm all alone with David. It's Jewel's day off, and— Oh, Ellie, I'm so scared. The factory's destroyed. The whole place's gone up in smoke. There's nothin' left 'cept a heap of black rubble. It's awful, just awful.' Her voice was muffled with weeping.

'Oh Shirlee, I'm so sorry. How did it happen?'

'I don't know. Sammy's there right now, finding out.'

Shocked at the hopelessness in her voice, I said, 'Listen, Shirlee, try to calm down. I'm coming over. I'll leave straight away.'

'Gee, thanks Ellie, I'm grateful.'

'What's up?' came Dora's anxious voice from the workroom as soon as I replaced the receiver.

'That was Shirlee. There was a fire at the factory last

night – it's burned to the ground. No one was hurt, but she's desperately upset.'

'Oh my Lordy!' Dora cried. 'You'd think some of my family would have phoned to tell me.'

'I'm sure they will. I'm going over to her. You'll manage for a couple of hours on your own, won't you?'

'Sure. I'll be fine.'

I hurried upstairs, changed into my suit, and rushed off, calling goodbye after me. I couldn't imagine that the factory was gone. It didn't seem possible until I got there and saw for myself the blackened ruin basking in the sunshine, its jagged walls jutting up in the air like broken limbs, holes where the windows once had been, workmen milling around it.

Shirlee, shading her eyes with the brim of her hat, was standing in the yard, weeping. 'It's all gone – destroyed,' she sobbed plaintively.

In that moment it seemed as if our past had gone up in smoke as, arm in arm, we stood and stared at the heap of rubble and ash that had been the entrance. All that was left of Mr Samuel's office were four charred walls, gaping up at the sky. It didn't seem possible that so much destruction could happen in one night without it being noticed.

I gazed at the mangled clothes racks strewn among the debris and pictured the beautiful crisp shirts that had dangled from them, heard the sound of Miss Flint, the floor manager, shouting to us girls to start packing them up for delivery; and heard the whirr of the sewing machines, and Dora and Wilma's laughter above the din at something funny Shirlee had said. The now-charred wall in the yard was where we used to eat our sandwiches while we mapped out our glorious futures. Shirlee with her secret smile, determined to win Mr Samuel's heart.

'Remember the day before the holidays, throwing our overalls up in the air, rushing out the door to endless days of doing nothing but havin' a good time,' Shirlee sniffed.

'Happy days,' I said to her.

Mr Samuel emerged from the rubble, looking pale and drawn. Shirlee went to him, and threw her arms around him. 'Oh, Sammy. What're we going to do?' she sobbed afresh.

'I don't know, honey,' he said in a deadpan voice, shaking her arms off gently, removing his panama hat as if in tribute to his dead factory.

'I'm so sorry about the fire, Mr Samuel,' I said in a choking voice.

'Thanks, Ellie. Would you mind taking Shirlee home, please – stay with her till I get back?'

'Of course I will.'

'I'll get dinner going,' Shirlee said, putting her hand on his arm, but he shrugged her off, lost in his worries.

'Count me out, I'm not hungry,' he said absently, and went off to have a look round.

We stepped back. I took Shirlee's arm and we made our way slowly to her car.

It was dark when Mr Samuel finally came home. Pale as a ghost, his eyes glazed over, he came into the lounge, and slumped down heavily into an armchair.

'Everything's gone. They didn't manage to salvage a thing,' he said, sounding exhausted.

'Did you find out how the fire got started?' Shirlee asked him.

'Nope. Wouldn't be surprised if someone set it alight deliberately,' he said.

'Why would anyone want to do a thing like that?' she asked, amazed.

'Any number of reasons – there're the rivals wanting to take our share of the business for one. Not that I have anything to prove it, but I have my suspicions. Oh, and by the way, don't go there again, it's dangerous now it's just a heap of old rubble,' he said, casting me a sidelong look.

'Did you talk to the insurance company?' Shirlee asked.

'I did, and they were most uncooperative. I lost my rag with them. We had a sort of a row.'

'You got into a fight with the insurance people?'

Mr Samuel turned impatiently. 'It wasn't a fight, more of a disagreement. They kept asking stupid questions. But I'll have my guys work it out.'

A car swept up outside.

'It's the police,' Shirlee said, taken aback.

'More damned questions.' Mr Samuel sighed, got to his feet. 'You stay here, Shirlee, and don't worry your pretty little head. I'll smooth things over.' As he went to answer the door a shifty flicker came into his eyes.

We heard voices and footsteps as they made their way to his study at the rear of the house. Shirlee looked scared as she said, 'I wouldn't wonder if he blames himself for what happened. The factory's been his whole life since he was a boy. Without it he's nothing.' Her voice cracked. 'He spent most of his time in it.'

I didn't think it was a good time to mention his endless golf outings and fishing trips.

'Sometimes I thought it was all too much for him, especially lately when business slackened.'

I looked at her in surprise.

'Oh things have been goin' downhill lately, and Sammy hasn't been himself. When he is home he spends most of his time in his study. It's his refuge from the outside world. I don't know where he goes in the evenings, and when I wake up in the night and he's not in yet I feel so alone. I don't know much about what goes on in his life any more. We don't entertain like we used to and he doesn't come anywhere with David and me these days,' she said sadly. 'I know things ain't easy and he's got a lot on his mind . . .'

For the first time I began to wonder if Mr Samuel had

set the factory alight himself to claim the insurance. That thought didn't seem to have crossed Shirlee's mind, so instead of voicing it I said, 'He loves you and little David, Shirlee, I know he does,' to console her.

'Yeah, I know, but sometimes I look in the mirror and I don't recognise myself. It's a strange feeling, Ellie, but I'm not the same person I was.' She dropped her voice. 'Sammy doesn't even approve of me takin' David to the park alone. He says that's what he's payin' Jewel for. He even suggested that I stop going there, but I like meetin' the other moms. It's something to dress up for.' Her face crumpled suddenly into grief. 'It was all so different when we first got together.'

She looked reflective, thinking of the man she'd fallen for, and I didn't know what to say.

'I lie awake at night next to him and think that I'm just a face and a voice to him. Nothing special, just someone he's gotten used to. He doesn't really know me, and I don't know him any more either. It frightens me, Ellie, I mean suppose I was out somewhere and I met a different person, a man that I liked, that paid me a little attention. Or if he met someone else . . .' Her voice trailed off.

'Don't think like that. You love him, Shirlee, don't you?'

'Sure I do. What girl wouldn't? A handsome, well-to-do man like him. Oh, what did I think I was doin' when I set my sights on him? Maybe I shouldn't have set my cap so high.' She rubbed her eyes thoughtfully. 'I never mentioned to you before that when I brought him home to meet my folks they all sat there staring at him. Pa said that I was far too young for him. My aunts reckoned that I must be pregnant – how else would I have snared him? Mom stuck up for me. She told them that he was my choice and that was the end of it.' She smiled suddenly through her tears. 'Oh, Ellie, I should have married a rodeo bull rider, someone wild. Sammy's too much of a businessman for me. If only I'd done more with my life, got an education. But I was crazy to get away from home, and get a job to help Mom out.' Tired, she lay back. 'Oh, listen to me goin' on, making a fool of myself. I should just have to remember all the good times Sammy and I have had.'

'And you will have again.'

She smiled and let her head tip back against the cushions. 'I should just loll around all day reading trashy books, not bother trying to keep up with Sammy and his lifestyle all the time. It's wearing me out.'

On the spur of the moment I said, 'Shirlee, would you consider coming to work for me in the store – just mornings? There're times when Dora and I are so busy there's no one to attend to the customers.'

It seemed an absurd idea, but Shirlee sat up, interested. 'Oh, Ellie, I'd sure love to, but Sammy wouldn't hear of it, I don't think, do you?' she said doubtfully.

'You won't know until you ask him. I'm sure he'll be

fine about it, once he knows that David is safe and happy with Jewel. Tell him it's just for the company, that you're lonely in the daytime.'

She was thoughtful for a moment. 'Jewel is wonderful with David you know, and he loves her. Oh Ellie, wouldn't it be fun!'

There was a shuffling in the hall and the front door banged as the police left, waking David up. When Jewel brought him downstairs, Shirlee lifted him on to her lap and cuddled him. His golden head glinted in the evening sun that slanted through the windows as he settled into her arms.

'Shirlee, Mr Samuel needs you right now, just as much as David does. You're the centre of the family, an excellent mother to David.' It was the truth. Shirlee *was* a great mother. She spent a lot of time with David, made certain that his manners were correct, and reminded him of who he was regularly, and that he must live up to his name.

On the way home I wondered again if Mr Samuel had actually burned down his factory. Shirlee had said he was in trouble financially, and he certainly didn't seem all that upset about it. I decided not to think about it in case I let my suspicions slip to Shirlee. She'd be devastated if it were true. Instead, I thought of the fun we'd have if Shirlee came to work with me, and felt uplifted.

Nine

True to his word, Mr Samuel took care of everything, and before long suitable premises were found near the old factory, and soon he was settled in.

One day out of the blue he phoned me.

'Ellie, I'd like you to come and see me . . . to talk over something,' he said. His tone was serious – which wasn't his style at all.

Surprised at this unusual request, and filled with curiosity, I went to see him.

Wreathed in smiles, he greeted me and took me into his office, where he sat down behind an enormous desk like a king on a throne, and came straight to the point. 'Sit down, Ellie. I've asked you here because I need your help.'

'Mine?' Surprised, I looked at him.

He leaned forward. 'I've found just what I've been looking for,' he said excitedly. 'There's a sportswear manufacturers for sale – name of Go-Go, it's an old, well-established brand. I thought that if I can get it for the right price I could update it – and with your flair in design, put my own special mark on the label.'

I was so taken back I said, 'Is this a joke, Mr Samuel?'

'No it certainly is not. This matter is far too important to me to joke about,' he said crossly.

'But I've only ever designed hats.'

'It wouldn't be that different. With a little stretch of the imagination and that wonderful style of yours, you could work wonders with clothes, Ellie.'

I bit my lip. 'I'm not so sure, Mr Samuel. It seems like a very big deal to me. Don't get me wrong, I'm very grateful, but I'm not sure I'm up to it, and there's my own business to think of.'

My doubts didn't put him off. 'It's a golden opportunity for you to stretch your imagination.' Seeing that I was still doubtful he said, 'You know there are lots of good designers out there who'd jump at this opportunity, but I thought I'd give you a chance.' He sat back to let that statement sink in.

'What about my hats?'

'My designs wouldn't take up too much of your time – you can continue with them. Take on an apprentice when you get busier. I'll pay her wages.'

'What would be involved?' I asked tentatively.

'Ellie, the sportswear trade needs a kick into the future. It's too conservative in this day and age of liberation. It's all about safe designs. Here look at these.'

He showed me photographs of models wearing the kinds of ugly, wool jersey bathing suits that I was familiar with; the legs to mid-thigh and beneath them modesty shorts in patterns or stripes.

'I'd like to have a women's sportswear fashion division, that's where you come in,' he enthused.

'Practical clothes that allow for movement,' I suggested.

'Yes, I want to bring sportswear into the Roaring Twenties, not just with feminine bathing suits, but also with shorter skating and tennis skirts in cotton or rayon. See, physical fitness is becoming important in Europe. So my aim is to make women's ready-to-wear sports garments that'd sell over the US,' he said enthusiastically.

'That's a very big deal.'

'I know, but it makes sense.'

Shaking my head I said, 'I don't know if I'm the one who could help you pull it off.'

'Listen, Ellie, you're proving to be a bit of a genius with your hat designs, and you've got vision. I spotted that when you worked in my shirt factory. You could do wonders with any kind of material, given the chance; you're a smart young woman. You have an eye for trends. I know that women would want to buy your designs.' And let's face it, the future is in ready-to-wear garments that the working girl can afford to buy, the made-to-measure trade is only for wealthy ladies. I want designs that are comfortable and easy to wear, and reasonably priced, but with a kind of elegance.'

'Isn't that asking for the moon?' I laughed.

'No, I'd use cheaper materials like this new rayon – it's so versatile.'

'It's something I'd give my right arm to do but . . .'

'There's a new French designer by the name of Coco Chanel, who is designing wonderful clothes in Paris.' Mr Samuel looked at me from under his dark eyelashes and smiled softly. 'You could learn from her,' he continued.

'Yes, I've seen some of her glorious hats in Macy's.' I'd also seen her grey crêpe pantalets with stiffly-tied aeroplane bows, and chiffon frocks with butterfly wings floating from the shoulders.

He nodded. 'And her beachwear's something else too. The French women are slavishly following her style.'

'I heard that she's become immensely successful.'

'Yes, she has.' There was a glint in Mr Samuel's eye as he said, 'What would you say if I offer to take you to Paris with me to the Exposition of Decorative Arts, somewhere you will see the greatest fashions of this century.'

'Paris!' I stuttered. 'You'd take me to Paris? Is that what you're saying?' I looked at him, more baffled than ever.

'Sure, I'm going to see what's happening in fashion over there.' I felt the room swaying and had to grip my chair to steady myself.

'I don't believe it.'

'Perhaps you'll believe it when we land on French soil.'

Shocked and thrilled all at once, I said, 'What does Shirlee say about all this?'

'She's happy to go along with anything I want to do. She has confidence in my ideas, and she knows what great talent you've got.'

'Is she coming to Paris with us?'

'No, I'd sure love to bring her with me, but with the new baby and all it wouldn't be safe for her to travel right now.'

'Would she object to me going?'

'No, of course not.' He paused. 'Does that mean you agree to give it a go?' he then added. He settled back in his chair, and said, in a more confidential tone, 'I don't want to go ahead unless I've got you on board.' I smiled at his persistence. Nothing, it seemed, was going to put him off this idea.

'Thank you for your confidence in me,' I said, not wanting to seem ungrateful, and glowing from his approval.

He flashed his most engaging smile as he stood up. 'It's a sudden decision, I know, but I believe in striking while the iron is hot. I'll ring Go-Go and make them an offer.'

He looked preoccupied for a moment, and then he glanced at his watch. 'Oh, I must be off. I promised Shirlee I'd be home on time this evening. Come on, I'll give you a lift.'

It was only when I was about to climb out of the passenger seat of his glorious motorcar that I realised that he hadn't once mentioned a salary. 'You haven't mentioned money, Mr Samuel.'

'That's true.' He looked reflective for a moment before he said, 'I'd pay you well, you know that.'

'I'd have to have something more pinned down than that.'

'Like what?'

'I'm not sure. I'll talk to Zak, he's my financial adviser.'

Mr Samuel raised his eyebrows in surprise, then gave a throaty laugh as he glanced across at me. For a moment he didn't seem to trust himself to speak. 'I hadn't bargained for this.' Frowning, he gave me a long, careful look, pursed his lips. 'I've been terribly overburdened lately, what with the fire and everything.'

'You can't expect to get me too cheaply.' I pressed on. 'I'll call Zak, see what he thinks.'

After a pause he said, 'OK, do that, and get back to me after the weekend.'

Later, when I was alone, I was struck by the enormity of Mr Samuel's proposal. I kept asking myself whether his ideas were too far-fetched. But the more I thought about them the more excited I became about the venture. Thinking of Coco Chanel's fabulous designs gave me a thrilling sensation and such a burst of inspiration and energy that I felt I might explode if I didn't get something down on paper.

I made myself a cup of coffee, took out my sketchpad

and, seated at the kitchen table, began sketching a cotton printed bathing suit with a little overskirt, then a more daring one with a cut-out section in the midriff panel. Next I sketched a figure-hugging bathing costume, cut higher on the legs, with the back scooped out, so that women could show off their tans at night in backless evening dresses. I added a bathing cap similar to a cloche but without the brim.

I sketched widely-flared trousers in sailor style to be made up in crêpe-de-chine and worn with blue-and-white tops or short jackets. How would Mr Samuel like these, I wondered, as I set to work on a skating skirt, making it shorter than ever before, and a pair of tennis shorts with matching top. There would be beach wraps, floppy sun hats, and fine knitted bathing suits to match. Pleased with the result, I phoned Zak.

'I need your advice, Zak,' I said after a little small talk. There was a pause.

'Oh,' Zak said in a surprised voice.

Briefly, I told him about Mr Samuel's proposition. '. . . And he's offered to take me to Paris to see the latest fashions there. What do you think? Should I do it? And what sort of payment should I ask for?'

Zak chuckled. 'Steady on, I can only answer one question at a time. It sounds like a great idea, but I'd have to know more about it before I could give you an opinion as to what to charge him. Tell you what. Why don't we all meet here to discuss it – say

Wednesday evening? I can get Dinah to check if Mr Samuel is free.'

Zak, elegant in a charcoal three-piece suit, matched with a white shirt and blue silk tie, was smiling broadly as he came to greet me. 'Hi Ellie, come in, sit down,' he said, pulling out a chair in front of his desk.

'I have something to show you.' I took out my sketchpad, and handed it to him.

He whistled under his breath. 'I say, these are really something!'

'Why, thank you.'

'How do you feel about such a challenge?'

'To be honest I feel it's all too much at once, and I'd still be working with Mr Samuel and not pursuing my independence.'

'It wouldn't be the same as when you worked in the shirt factory. You'd design at home. Think of the endless possibilities this business would hold for you. Opportunities like this don't come along very often.'

It was as if the whole world was at my feet. Mr Samuel arrived and, very composed, shook hands with us both.

'Ellie told me all about your new venture, congratulations,' Zak said.

'Yes, I'm really excited about this,' Mr Samuel agreed. 'It's got right under my skin.'

'Ellie's very excited about it too.'

'I've made a few sketches,' I said, handing them to Mr Samuel.

His face lit up. 'Wow! With designs like these we could go far, Ellie.'

'I agree,' Zak declared as he settled back in his chair.

'And what would you know about the rag trade?' asked Mr Samuel brusquely.

'Nothing about the clothes, but everything about the financial end of it, that's why I'm here – to protect Ellie's interests. Do you mind if I ask you some questions?'

I could feel the tension between them as their eyes locked. 'Certainly, go ahead. I've no objection,' Mr Samuel said, stiffly.

'Tell me about this company you're thinking of buying.'

'It's an old family business founded in the 1850s by two brothers who came from England and settled here in Boston. They manufacture very outdated sportswear and casual wear, and the brothers are too old to modernise.'

'Is it solid financially?'

Mr Samuel's eyes were steely. 'Mr Rubens, I've been in the rag trade long enough to know a bargain when I see one. There are a lot of manufacturers who would jump at the chance to buy it. And besides, my lawyer's looked into it. Says it's in good shape, and I'm getting it at a good price.' Reluctantly, he handed papers over to Zak, who laid them down before him and sat reviewing the figures, making notes in a small notebook.

'This factory has terrific potential for Ellie,' Mr Samuel continued, while Zak was absorbed in the figures. 'With my expertise, and her flair for fashion, we could turn it around, bring it into the twentieth century. I'm planning on building up a strong ready-to-wear market to sell to retail outlets.'

'It makes a lot of sense,' Zak said. 'So let's suppose that you do buy it – would you be the only shareholder?'

'Oh no, there'd be Shirlee, of course . . .'

Zak looked at him carefully. 'You wouldn't object then if Ellie had a stake in the company?'

This was something Mr Samuel hadn't bargained for. Baffled, he said, 'I don't think that's possible.'

'Well, it depends on what Ellie's designs are worth to you?' Zak asked.

'Oh, I'm prepared to pay good money for them.'

'Of course, but Ellie wouldn't consider selling them.'

I looked at Zak in amazement.

'She wouldn't?' Mr Samuel was taken aback.

'No, I think you'll have to come up with a better offer than that. Why not make Ellie a shareholder? With a small stake in the business she could draw dividends, receive company reports and balance sheets. And, then, when the company is making money, she could also draw a salary from it.'

'Oh no, I couldn't do that.' Mr Samuel was horrified.

Undaunted, Zak pressed on. 'As chairman of the board

and major shareholder, you'll have the power to do anything you wish with the company.' Zak's eyes swept over him. 'It seems to me that you can't afford not to make Ellie a shareholder. Look at it this way. You need her far more than she needs you. Isn't it better to give her shares than be without her?' he said forcefully. Startled, I looked up. 'Isn't that right, Ellie?' Zak was settled back in his chair, waiting for me to say something.

'Oh, yes,' I agreed. 'It's shares or nothing.' I was bowled over by the masterful way Zak had handled Mr Samuel, reeling him in like a fish on a line. Mr Samuel was thoughtful as he pondered what Zak had just said, and Zak waited, poised to meet fierce opposition. These two men understood one another, a passion for making money being their common ground.

Eventually Mr Samuel said, 'How about we say a stake of five per cent?'

'Make it ten.' Zak raised his eyebrows at me.

'She's only a kid!' Mr Samuel whined.

'If you were to employ a top, established designer it would cost you much more than that, as you well know.'

'OK, have it your way,' said a scowling Mr Samuel. 'I'll organise the papers.' He looked at me, as if expecting me to say something. I glanced across at Zak. He caught my eye and gave me a reassuring smile.

'I'll do my best not to disappoint you,' was all I could manage, the thought of this proposition and the possibilities it held for me were overwhelming.

Zak stood up. 'Well, that's it for the moment. I look forward to hearing from you when you have everything finalised.'

'OK,' Mr Samuel shot back. 'I'm going home to break the news to Shirlee.'

When the deal was done Mr Samuel invited Zak and I for supper to celebrate. Shirlee, looking rested and pretty as a picture, presided over a delicious meal. When we were on the lobster mornay Mr Samuel raised his glass of soda and proposed a toast. 'Welcome on to the board, Ellie.'

'To Ellie,' Zak and Shirlee chorused.

Zak's eyes shone, his skin glowed as he said, 'And here's to your trip to Paris. I'm sure it'll be a wonderful experience for both of you.'

Shirlee frowned as if she hadn't quite heard correctly. 'What did you say?'

Mr Samuel smiled sheepishly. 'Oh heck! Didn't I tell you? I'm taking Ellie to Paris with me.'

We all fell silent at the look on Shirlee's face. 'So you didn't feel the need to talk to me about it first?'

'It's no big deal – you can't travel at the moment, you said so yourself.'

'And you're quite happy to leave me here all by myself while you and Ellie clear off to enjoy yourselves?'

'What do you expect me to do? Let's enjoy our meal, honey, we'll talk later,' Mr Samuel said. Turning to Zak, he continued talking about the business.

Shirlee put down her knife and fork, and cleared her throat. 'I suppose you're gonna pretend everything's OK? Well it ain't. I never imagined you could do something like this to me.'

'Shirl, calm down, and let's enjoy our dinner.'

She grabbed the water jug and flung its contents over Mr Samuel.

He jumped up. 'What'd you do that for?'

She turned to me. 'This is all your doing! You tricked him into taking you to Paris, made it part of the deal no doubt,' she cried.

Flabbergasted, I said, 'That's not true, Shirlee.'

'She did no such thing, Shirlee,' Zak said.

'And what would you know about our business?' she retorted. 'You're just a soulless rich guy. You don't give a damn about us or Ellie or anyone as long as you get a cut of the deal.'

I covered my face with my hands, heaving with embarrassment.

'Quit this, Shirl.' Mr Samuel went to her, took her arm. 'Come on, we'll go upstairs, talk about it. Excuse us, kids. Won't be long.' They left the room, Shirlee walking meekly beside Mr Samuel, her hands trembling.

'What was all that about?' asked a shaken Zak.

'It's not like Shirlee. I do know she's very unsettled right now.'

Zak got to his feet, walked around the table looking

like a caged lion. 'I think we should go, leave them to it,' he suggested.

'What! Now? We can't just walk out – shouldn't we at least wait to say goodbye?'

'No, Ellie, we'll only be an embarrassment to them if we stay on. You can always phone Shirlee tomorrow and have a talk.'

'OK.'

We left quietly.

'Mr Samuel was inconsiderate not to have told Shirlee about the trip to Paris before, with her feeling so insecure right now,' I said as we shot off down the drive.

'I think he was downright cruel and who could blame her for being upset, stuck at home while you'll be having the time of your lives,' Zak said.

'I doubt that, we'll be working hard.'

'But Paris is such an exciting city.' He shot a glance at me. 'And you'd better get used to all that if you're going to make it big in the rag trade.'

His words excited me but I felt too worried about Shirlee to let myself get carried away. Did she really believe that I'd forced Mr Samuel to invite me to Paris? Or was it something she just blurted out on the spur of the moment?

As Zak bade me goodnight I wished he'd take me in his arms and kiss me, if only to comfort me. But all he said was 'See you soon' and drove off. Romance seemed to be the last thing on his mind.

The next day when I telephoned Shirlee, Jewel answered and said that she was resting, and didn't wish to be disturbed. She didn't return my call. I wrote a note to her to let her know that I wouldn't go to Paris if it would cause her that much distress, and how I hated this falling out, if that's what it was. When I didn't hear back I went to see Mr Samuel to tell him that I wouldn't be travelling with him.

'Gee, Ellie! Don't let Shirlee put you off. The pregnancy's making her feel lousy right now. She'll come round. She'll be fine about it. She thinks the world of you, you know that.' Taking out his diary, he glanced at it. 'We'll arrive in time for the big Chanel fashion show. Bring your evening gown.'

The reason he gave for Shirlee's behaviour seemed plausible, but when she didn't get in touch before we left for Paris I guessed that she still wasn't 'fine about it' at all, and Mr Samuel had only said it to keep me happy.

Ten

The city of Paris twinkled in the misty twilight as dusk descended upon it like a curtain. Mr Samuel pointed out the Eiffel Tower, festooned with lights, and the giant floodlit Arc de Triomphe monument. I caught my breath in wonder as we whirled out on to the busy Champs Elysées, a glittering avenue of colourful stores and glinting windows behind slanting trees, and crossed the shimmering River Seine.

Down the Left Bank, the magnificent façades of buildings were shrouded in a blue hue. Then we were outside the majestic Ritz hotel, in the Place Vendôme, ablaze with light from its long sash windows.

Mr Samuel helped me out of the taxi and led me up the steps, through the portico and into a glorious gilded lobby where clerks stood rigidly behind desks, and bellboys rushed around after the fur-clad ladies amid greetings of 'How are you? What a lovely surprise! Can't wait to see the show!'

Eventually a bellhop led the way to the lift and we

floated up to the top floor to two small but beautiful rooms side by side.

After a hot, scented bath, I dressed in the black frock Violet had bought for me, twisted my hair up in a neat chignon, and went to join up with Mr Samuel, who led me down a sumptuous long gallery to the bar to the sound of a string quartet playing 'I Love Paris in the Springtime'. There, among men in dress suits and glamorous women, his eyes roamed around like a secret agent's until they rested on a tall, sophisticated, dark-haired lady, standing to one side.

'Françoise!' he called to her.

'Sammy!'

He made his way to her, me close behind. 'So good to see you again,' he said, inclining his head reverentially.

'Enchanté,' she gushed, the scent of her glorious perfume rising into the air as he lifted her hand to kiss it.

Turning to me, he said importantly, 'Eleanor, I'd like you to meet my very good friend, Madame Marchant, one of the top designers at the House of Chanel.'

'I'm very pleased to meet you,' I said, almost bowing before her.

She shook my hand briefly, her haughty eyes never leaving Mr Samuel's. 'I'm here with guests, do join us for dinner.' A distinguished man caught her attention. 'Alain,' she beckoned. 'You remember Sammy, don't you?'

'Of course.' The men clasped hands.

Mr Samuel called the bartender and ordered cocktails for everyone. A beautiful young woman with a white poodle strode by.

'Judging by the style of the young women, there's quite a bit of money about,' Mr Samuel said casually.

'She's one of the Rothschilds, leads a crazy life,' Madame said behind her hand.

'These rich people know how to spend,' said the man called Alain.

Two beautiful French girls joined us, and we all filed into the restaurant. I sat on tenterhooks at a long table lined with flowers and fruit, comparing their confidence with my uncertainty, but they lightened the mood with their friendly chatter, telling us, in broken English, that they were dancers with the corps de ballet. When I told them that I was a milliner, one of them said, 'Americans do not know 'ow to wear 'ats. They are too formal. 'Ere we wear them to one side, and they look wonderful,' making me laugh, easing the tension.

The conversation flowed as waiters scurried around us. Mr Samuel, flushed like a schoolboy, enquired of Madame Marchant if he would be having the pleasure of her company at the new salon grand opening, saying, 'I was hoping that we might see something of one another, Françoise.' She pouted regretfully, telling him that she was off to Milan the following morning to one of the fashion houses there. 'Why don't you come to

Milan instead?' she said encouragingly. 'It's buzzing with fashion icons.'

'I can't, honey. I'll be heavily involved here with orders and sales people – and there's Miss O'Rourke,' he said, glancing slyly at me. His growing discontent because he wasn't getting anywhere with her was obvious.

'There's a great show in Monte Carlo. A group of us are going down there – lots of pretty girls,' Alain said to him.

'Can't make it.' Mr Samuel shook his head sadly.

Madame Marchant excused herself before dessert and left. Mr Samuel's eyes followed her. I think he liked her a lot.

After dinner we made our way to the great crystal ballroom where the fashion experts of the world were gathered, and took our seats among dark, handsome men and exquisitely-groomed women to watch a parade of radiant models swaying with confidence along the catwalk in cerise, mauve, and pink sheaths that fell away from their slim, perfect bodies in the new, longer length. More models appeared and moved around in elegant black-and-white evening gowns, and long white gloves that added drama to their look.

Excitement mounted into suspense as we waited, hoping for at least a glimpse of the elusive Coco Chanel. She appeared briefly on the catwalk to receive a bouquet of flowers. She was a small woman with luminous eyes and dark sleek hair. She wore one of her famous suits and lots of fake jewellery. I gazed at her in admiration, knowing that it must have taken a great deal of hard work and vitality to bring about a fashion show such as we'd just seen. She'd started out poor, equipped with only her love of fashion, her ambition, a talented pair of hands, and a calculating mind; she'd become France's top fashion designer. I wondered if, like me, escape had motivated her.

Afterwards, in the salon, the men floated about the tables talking delightedly about the clothes. A woman with a Pekinese dog came over to Mr Samuel. 'I say, fancy running into you!' she said, making her way over.

'Adele.' Their laughter filled the room as they greeted one another. I pleaded exhaustion and went to bed, glad to get away from them.

I opened the bedroom window and stared out at the full moon suspended above a myriad of twinkling stars, thinking of the wonderful clothes I'd just seen, breathing in the cool, Parisian air.

The next morning, after breakfast in bed, I made it to the nearby park. The grass was baked from the heat, flowers exploded in the flowerbeds, and birds chirped. A model in a cloud of pink chiffon, silk roses at her waist, and a gold straw sun hat, was being photographed.

'Stand still,' the photographer said, snapping away. 'Now move slowly towards me.' She moved gracefully, hair falling forward casting her face in shadow. I watched her, longing to design clothes like the dress she was wearing. To be part of that world.

On the way back to the hotel I stopped to buy a postcard to send to Alice and a copy of *Paris Match*. The cover photograph showed some of the models of the previous night's fashion show in their Chanel sheaths. The headline predicted that *This simple sheath is a winner* and that the future of clothes was *in mass-produced convenience*. There was no doubt but that Mr Samuel had the right idea.

He was waiting for me when I got back. 'I have an important meeting all day, so I've arranged for my friend, Pierre Clermont, to look after you. Ah, here he is now.'

I turned to see a tall, exquisitely-dressed young man in a grey suit coming towards us.

'Pierre, this is Ellie. Ellie, meet Pierre Clermont.'

'Enchanté! I am all yours.' The brilliance of his turquoise eyes and his warm smile made me catch my breath as we shook hands.

'Bonjour,' was all I managed to say, hardly believing my good fortune at having such a handsome escort.

Mr Samuel wasted no more time on pleasantries and with a wave of his hand he was gone.

'Have you known Mr Samuel long?' I asked, just to hear that beautiful accent of his again.

He smiled. 'We've worked together in the past.'

'Oh, so you're a fashion designer?'

'That is so. And you are a milliner I'm told.'

'That's right.'

'Well, we should have a lot to talk about. As you know, fashion is big business here in Paris.' He oozed self-confidence as he took my arm and steered me out of the hotel lobby door.

'Do you live in Paris?' I asked him on our way to the salon.

'Yes, but I spend a lot of time in the States. I thought I might show you the sights. Then we shall have lunch, and some good wine and good conversation?'

'Sounds wonderful.'

We walked past beautiful eighteenth-century mansions and Fouquets to the corner of the Rue de la Boetie, the street where the city's fashionable art galleries were. Under the Grand Palais's domed glass roof we looked at paintings of Max Ernst and Fernand Leger, Pierre's favourite artists.

Under the chestnut trees on the Avenue des Champs Elysées, we watched enormous glass fountains play among life-sized cubist dolls, and river barges sailing lazily beneath their glittering cascade of light.

From Montmartre we went up the Rue Pigalle into the Place Blanche. Pierre pointed out displays of abstract designs of the new art deco style on the way. We climbed up the steps of the Sacre Coeur, where the city shone in the sunlight. It was magical standing there, breathing in the air, quiet except the distant muffled traffic.

'It's like being on another planet,' I said, listening to the sound of the water that washed down from huge towers in the distance. Over lunch at a nearby café I asked Pierre to tell me about Coco Chanel.

He smiled. 'She's funny, and beautiful in her own way, and her soirees are notorious in Paris. Everyone wants an invitation. She's really quite wonderful, a great businesswoman of course, though she frightens the models sometimes when she shouts at them.'

'Is she married?'

'No, she is in love with the Duke of Westminster, the richest man in England, and he with her.'

'Oh, how thrilling.'

'Yes, but it is doomed, I fear. You see she won't give up her business for him, no matter what.' He paused for a second or two, then, 'Would you like to come to one of her soirees tomorrow night? There is a private viewing for some close friends.'

'Could I? It would be a dream come true.'

'I can easily arrange it.'

'What about Mr Samuel? He'll want to come too.'

'Of course I'll include him.' He smiled.

'How marvellous!' I said delightedly, trying not to sound too grateful.

We walked back slowly to the hotel. In the lobby I thanked Pierre for a lovely time, telling him how much I had enjoyed his company.

'And I yours, thank you, Ellie . . .' He lifted my hand and kissed it. 'A demain,' he murmured as we parted.

Eleven

After breakfast the next morning I spent at least an hour in front of the mirror trying on all of my frocks for the soiree that evening. They all looked positively dowdy compared to the simple little Chanel dresses I'd seen everywhere. Then, inspired, I suddenly had the idea to snip the flounces and frills off of my white broderie anglaise frock and trim the bodice with black ribbon instead. The result was a smooth sheath that showed off my figure and looked arresting.

The concierge told me where to find the nearest haberdashery. It was full of the most glorious trims I'd ever seen. There, I bought black ribbon with a glorious sheen on it, and hurried back to finish my alterations. Like a child, I ran to the mirror and was thrilled with the result. It was perfect and showed off my curves beautifully.

Satisfied, I gathered up my coat and purse and hurried to catch up with Mr Samuel for a day of business meetings.

★ ★ ★

After an exciting but stressful day of meetings with designers in fashion houses, Mr Samuel and I returned to the hotel exhausted, but excited about the evening ahead of us.

Later, in my revamped dress, black high-heels, sheer black stockings, and evening bag to match, I felt very grown up and sophisticated.

Mr Samuel was waiting for me in the lobby. 'I'm so nervous,' I told him as we drove off.

'Nonsense, you look delightful – but don't you have any jewellery to wear?' he asked. When I told him that I had nothing that would match my dress he said, 'Wait there, I'll get you something.' Off he went only to return a few minutes later with a necklace of jet beads.

'Where did you get them?' I gasped in delight as he clasped them around my neck.

'Borrowed them from a friend. Now have you got your notebook to make a note of all the fashions while I circulate, Ellie?'

'Yes, Mr Samuel.'

Pierre arrived. Immaculate in a satin evening suit, silver shirt and tie to match, his hair brushed back neatly, he looked both sophisticated and important.

'Ellie, you look wonderful,' he said, taking my hand and kissing it, before turning to greet Mr Samuel.

'Shall we go?' Mr Samuel asked, impatient to be off.

★　★　★

A doorman greeted us at the entrance to the Chanel mansion in Rue Faubourg St Honore and led us through a long chain of rooms divided by tall screens, and filled with satin sofas, and satin walls to match, that finally opened on to a garden full of beautiful people.

It was like stepping into fairyland. Candlelights twinkled in the garden. A piano player tinkled out a ragtime tune and Coco Chanel, sophisticated in a dark blue suit trimmed with white, and ropes of imitation pearls, came towards us and greeted Pierre in French.

As soon as he introduced us to her, Mr Samuel said, 'I'm so thrilled to meet you, Mademoiselle Chanel,' bowing so low over her hand that he almost fell.

When she turned to me I plucked up the courage to say, 'I greatly admire your designs.'

'Eleanor is a milliner,' Pierre explained to her.

'So young!' Her eyes on me were intense beneath her dark eyebrows as she took me to one side. 'Always remember that a woman's education consists of two lessons: never to leave the house without stockings, and never, ever to go out without a hat.'

'I couldn't agree with you more,' I said delightedly.

'Good.' She nodded and went off.

Platters heaped with hors d'oeuvres were served by white-coated waiters.

An important-looking lady in a fabulous black ruffled cocktail frock waved to Pierre. He gave her a brilliant smile as he waved back.

'I'm scared to death,' I said, taking in the fabulous scene unfolding.

'You'll be safe with me,' he laughed, taking my arm protectively as we went to dine.

Seated at the head of a glittering table under the stars, surrounded by an adoring group of men who hung on her every word, Mr Samuel among them, Coco Chanel was in her element, and so was I. Between mouthfuls of delicious seared salmon and asparagus tips, Pierre told me anecdotes about his life in the fashion world. My nerves calmed down; I began to enjoy myself.

After the meal, people broke into little groups. Pierre poured out two cups of coffee and led me to a seat under a willow tree. 'So, tell me what kind of hats you make,' he said.

'I try to make the hats look different and yet just right so that every woman in America will want to buy them.' I found myself confiding in him that I found it hard, being so young. 'It holds me back. I find that buyers in the big stores don't take me seriously enough.'

Pierre looked amused. 'But, that's wonderful. It's only in America that you would have the freedom to do that. Listen, Ellie, it may take you a little while but you'll get there because you're a wonderful, unspoilt, and exciting person. People will find themselves attracted to you, and your hats no doubt, and once you learn to trust in your own judgement, and not care about anyone else's opinions, you'll be fine.'

'Not care what anyone thinks?' I was shocked.

He nodded. 'I used to believe everything everyone said to me until I learned to be my own judge, and to stand on my own two feet, and not worry about what other people said or thought. There's only a certain amount of time you have to spend on other people's opinions, especially when you have better things to do. Believe me, I know. I grew up in the hard school of Chanel . . . Alors! Enough talk of shop, what do you like to do in your spare time? What music do you like? Who is your favourite film star?'

'I'm a jazz fan,' I said. 'Louis Armstrong is my favourite trumpeter.'

'Oh, so am I,' he said.

'And I love the movies.'

'You never know – Gloria Swanson could be at the show tonight! All the movie stars love Chanel.'

Under a cascade of brilliant lights, models with kohl eyes sailed up and down in swaying jersey dresses with pleated panels, and low-slung chiffon evening gowns with feather boas. They all had the Chanel trademark of casual elegance. From behind me I heard Coco hiss, 'Stand straight, girl,' at one of the models. 'Make the fabric move on the body.'

'Everything has to be exactly correct,' Pierre said under his breath. 'I try to tell her that they are only young girls doing their best, but she won't listen.' I sensed Pierre's frustration at Coco as he talked, but he was no match for her, and neither were any of the fawning men who flocked around her.

Then came the sportswear; black taffeta figure-hugging swimsuits worn with lots of jewellery, which was a great surprise. 'Chanel's strongest influence,' Alain informed us. 'She recommends it to be worn everywhere, even on the beach.'

There were clothes for watching sports in; country tweeds with ruffles and piping, so different to anything I'd ever seen before. When the procession ended the applause rose, and the models tossed their lovely heads in acknowledgement as they filed past.

As soon as the show was over Pierre drove us back to the hotel, where Mr Samuel bade us goodnight.

Alone, under the velvet stars, I told Pierre, 'It's been the most wonderful evening. I've had the time of my life.'

'You have made it a wonderful evening for me too, cherie,' he said, taking my hand, kissing it. 'Just watching you across the room was driving me wild,' he said in a lazy voice as he went to kiss me again.

'It's time I was going.' I pushed him away gently.

He tightened his grip. 'When am I going to have you to myself?'

'I'm here for another few days.'

'Perhaps tomorrow night?'

'I'll ask Mr Samuel.'

'Surely you can take an evening off without his

permission?' His hot breath was warm on my skin as he said persuasively, 'I'll be waiting for your answer.'

'Hi, Ellie! How're you doing?'

I turned at the sound of a familiar voice, to see Zak coming towards us. He looked tired but as handsome as ever.

'Zak! What are you doing here?'

'I was in London on business. Thought I'd take a little time out, hop over to see how you guys are doing. When I couldn't find you I went out for a stroll.' Zak smiled stiffly.

'But you never said . . .'

'It was a spur-of-the-moment decision. I'm entitled to time off occasionally,' he said, but even in the moonlight I noticed he coloured a little.

'Zak, this is Pierre Clermont,' I said, determined to put both of them at ease. 'He's a fashion designer with the House of Chanel.'

Zak held out his hand. 'I'm Zachary Rubens, Ellie's friend . . . and business associate. Pleased to make your acquaintance.'

They shook hands, and an uncomfortable silence followed.

'Would you like to come in for a drink?' Zak asked us.

Pierre shook his head. 'If you'll excuse me I must go, I have an early fashion shoot at the far side of Paris tomorrow.'

'Sure, nice to meet you.' Zak shook hands with him again. And with a 'tout à l'heure' to me, Pierre left.

In the lounge Zak ordered a nightcap and sat back, completely relaxed. 'I see you were in good company. The House of Chanel no less.'

'Oh, Zak, I had such a wonderful time at the show! It was the best experience I've ever had,' I told him.

'Really! And this Pierre – is he just as wonderful?'

'I hardly know him, but he seems to be a real gentleman.'

'You were flirting outrageously with him.' I heard the sharp tone to Zak's voice.

'No I wasn't,' I denied hotly. 'I was being gracious, as Mr Samuel expects me to be, and he thinks I'm handling myself very well.'

'That's because it suits him to have Pierre keeping you distracted while he flirts with all of the women. You're here on business, Ellie, remember?' he said sternly.

'Well, you don't have to worry about me, I'm doing fine,' I assured him crossly.

'Do you really believe that you're safe in the company of a Frenchman?'

'Of course I do.'

'Then you're a fool.' Zak gave a careless laugh but his eyes were intense. Could he be jealous? I wondered.

Just then Mr Samuel came strolling into the lounge, so deep in conversation with a glamorous woman that he didn't notice Zak and I.

'He's having a good time too, I see,' Zak said dryly.

'He's doing business.'

'Oh, sure,' he said sarcastically. 'Then he won't approve of me showing up like this, spoiling his pitch.'

I'd been thinking the same thing but I didn't dare say it.

He lowered his voice and said, 'He's a shark and don't you forget it, Ellie. You're dealing with a man who'd pull the wool over your eyes as quick as look at you.'

'He's been working very hard since we got here.' For some reason I felt the need to defend Mr Samuel.

'Look at you, I do believe you're angry.'

'Yes, I am. It's not fair to make assumptions like that when you don't know him very well.'

A shadow of confusion crossed Zak's face. 'Let's forget it, we won't let business interfere with the evening.' He held my gaze. 'If you think I'm here to spoil your fun you're wrong,' he said, but he sounded angry.

Mr Samuel spotted us and stared at Zak in surprise, then came over. As Zak got to his feet I rushed in to fill the gap. 'Zak decided to come and see how we were doing.'

'How thoughtless of me not to have invited you in the first place,' said Mr Samuel smoothly, his irritation barely hidden below the surface as he introduced Mademoiselle Fouchard, a buyer for Givenchy.

'Are you staying here?' Mr Samuel asked him.

'Sure am,' Zak said.

Zak was as polite as ever, offering them a drink, which they both declined. Once Madame Fouchard left the conversation became laboured, with Mr Samuel glancing at his watch and generally making it obvious that Zak was not welcome.

'You won't mind if I retire to bed? I have an early start in the morning – as has Ellie,' he added pointedly.

'Not at all.' Zak smiled graciously.

I felt tense and tired, and I rose from my seat. 'I'll say goodnight too, Zak. I hope you sleep well.' I followed Mr Samuel to the lift and left Zak staring after us.

'Did you know he was coming here?' Mr Samuel asked crossly as we floated upwards.

'No, it's just as much of a shock to me.'

'I wonder what he's after?'

'Nothing. He was in London, so he thought he'd come to see the exposition.'

Mr Samuel shook his head. 'I don't believe that for one moment.'

To our surprise, Zak appeared at the breakfast table the next morning. 'How long are you planning on staying?' Mr Samuel asked him rudely as soon as he sat down.

'Just a couple of days,' Zak said smoothly. 'I thought I might go to a couple of meetings with you, get acquainted with the fashion business while I'm here.'

'Come if you want but, I warn you, you'll be bored with the details.'

'Not at all, how's it going?'

'Fine. If it all works out according to plan we'll be making a comfortable living for at least the next few years.'

Observing them circle around one another during the day was fascinating. Zak wasn't afraid to challenge Mr Samuel – pulling him up on certain things, arguing with him about others, all done with enough delicacy to keep Mr Samuel calm and not let him feel that he was being interrogated.

That evening, Mr Samuel and I met Pierre in the bar. 'Where is your boyfriend?' Pierre asked, looking around.

'Zak's not my boyfriend, he's a business colleague,' I explained.

'Ah!' Pierre gave me a wry look. 'Then why's he so jealous of me?'

'Oh, he's not jealous. He's protective of me, that's all.'

Zak came sauntering in and came straight over. 'Is it OK if I take Ellie to dinner?' he asked Mr Samuel.

'Sure, be my guest.'

'Perhaps you should ask the lady first?' Pierre suggested.

'I was about to,' Zak snarled back. 'Ellie, would you like to have dinner with me?'

'I'd love to, but what about you, Pierre? Would you like to come with us?'

'No thank you,' he said stiffly. 'I must go make some calls. See you later, Ellie.'

It was a warm evening. The wide boulevards were filled with dappled sunlight; the smart café-restaurants shaded by plane trees.

'Paris is so grand,' Zak said, as we strolled along, stopping to browse at some rare antique china and glass in shop windows. We dined on the leafy terrace of Le Closeria des Lilas, a chic restaurant where artists dined and signed the tablecloths to pay for their meal.

'Dinner's so different when people wear formal clothes,' Zak said. 'This is better than any show.'

'Can I ask you something, Zak?'

'Sure.'

'Why did you really come here?'

He took a sip of his drink. 'I couldn't resist seeing Paris, and the sights,' he said boyishly.

'That's not the real reason.'

He nodded. 'Being truthful, I was anxious about you. I thought you might need a helping hand in dealing with Mr Samuel.' He looked vulnerable as he said, 'I needn't have worried. You look as if you're doing fine.'

'So, your trip was in vain?'

'Oh, no, not at all, I love Paris, and I'm happy with Mr Samuel's performance.'

'That's good.'

'Pierre Clermont is obviously happy too. He seems very taken with you.'

'Zak I—'

'He's not suitable for you, Ellie. Frenchmen aren't reliable, they get bored with women easily.'

'He's a colleague, Zak, nothing else,' I laughed.

Zak shot me a look of surprise. 'Oh Ellie, you're so naïve. I was right to be anxious about you.' There was a sharpness to his tone now that I'd never heard before.

After the meal Zak took my hand as we walked down the Boulevard Montparnasse. He stopped before we reached the Ritz. Suddenly, he drew me to him and enfolded me in his arms. 'You look so lovely tonight,' he said in a caressing tone. 'I've missed you, Ellie.'

'You have?'

'More than I ever thought I could.' He reached out, pulled me to him. 'That's why I'm here.'

I gazed up into his fiery eyes, spellbound, the desire for him sending the blood rushing to my head. He took me in his arms, kissed me slowly and tenderly. I was trembling, light-headed, the realisation that he wanted me sending an aching sensation through me. When I finally pulled away he looked at me with burning eyes. 'We'll be together one day, and nothing will keep us apart.'

I stepped back. 'But we come from such different backgrounds, Zak.'

'That'll all change. You'll become a brilliant fashion designer. You'll do it, I know you will.' He stopped, took a step closer. 'I want you to know that I'll be the first to applaud you. I care about you, Ellie. I've always cared about you, and don't you forget that.' He lifted my chin. 'I'll be gone when you wake up in the morning, so I'll say goodbye now.' He crushed me to him in a deep passionate embrace. 'See you in Boston,' he said and was gone.

I fell into bed, my mind full of Zak and the evening we'd spent together. I was his now. Nothing and no one could ever separate us again. We belonged together.

Twelve

As soon as I returned to Boston I began designing a range of wild and witty hats based on the ones I'd seen in Paris. Dora had been filling the shelves vacated by my designs with her own line of wholesale hats. I explained to Dora that I was creating a salon just like the ones I'd seen in Paris.

'How fancy,' she said, unimpressed. 'We have to have new rules. We have to have a contract.'

I told her that she was an employee, and would continue to be for the foreseeable future, but that in time we could work something out. I could tell by the way she gathered up an armful of hats and banged the door after her, that she thought I was developing ambitions above my station.

I wrote to Alice, telling her all about that wonderful city and promising to take her to see it one day. She wrote back:

Dear Ellie,

I want to come to Boston to live with you. I can't stand living here any more. Please send me the train fare as soon as you can. I'll be a great help to you and you won't regret it.

Your loving sister,

Alice

I replied, telling her that I would come for her as soon as I began to make some money from the sale of my new hats, and to try and be patient until then, and to do her best to get on with the family.

I was busy with the work and enjoying myself with Zak. It was like old times, going to jazz concerts with him and Violet. Sometimes, we would sneak away from the boisterous crowd and go off to the sea for a walk. Since our return from Paris we'd discovered a new kind of thrill in each other's company. And we had fun. It was as if the time we'd spent apart had made us appreciate one another all the more.

But when he told me about his plans to have his twenty-third birthday party at the family summerhouse in Hyannis Port my heart sank. I hadn't been in good shape the last time I'd stayed there.

'Cheer up, darling,' he said. 'It'll be great fun. I have a special surprise arranged.'

Zak took it for granted that I would fit in. It was easy to persuade me on a moonlit beach that it would be 'fun', but it turned out to be far from the case when Violet and I arrived in Hyannis Port.

It was strange to be back there again. The Rubens' summerhouse looked completely different. There was nothing of the quiet, lonely atmosphere of those miserable days I'd spent there on my own, waiting for Zak to return.

Pots of colourful flowers adorned the porch. A striped fabric tent ballooned over the wide lawn of their yard, and workmen were busy hauling tables and chairs into it.

'Oh, how romantic,' Violet exclaimed excitedly as we stepped out of her car, but I was a bundle of nerves as I followed her up the path.

Mrs Savino, the housekeeper, came running to the door before we had a chance to ring the bell.

'Ellie! I'm so glad to see you,' she cried, throwing her arms around me in a motherly hug, 'and you too, Violet,' she said, hugging her also. 'You're early. Come and have coffee. There's no one else about.'

The house was welcoming; every room filled with flowers, the patio doors thrown open wide. I walked out on to the stoop, thinking how strange it was to be back there again, and how different everything was since the time I'd sat there feeling so alone, and with the future so uncertain.

After coffee and a catch-up with Mrs Savino we went to our room to change for the party. It was the same room that I'd stayed in last time. We showered and changed into our dresses, mine pink-and-gold moiré, Violet's a long straight black Dior dress, a present from her mother. With her hair sleeked back she looked older and more beautiful, in her natural way.

I fumbled with the pins as I tried to put my hair up.

'Here, let me do it,' Violet said, taking the hairbrush from my hand and swishing it up with two sweeps, leaving a few tendrils hanging softly around the nape of my neck.

'I'm so nervous at the thought of meeting Zak's parents again,' I said shakily.

'Don't worry about them. They won't stay too long. They'll be whizzed off somewhere for a game of cards in one of the neighbours' houses as soon as the party gets started. There, have a look in the mirror,' she said, patting a couple of the pins into place.

I couldn't believe the difference. Not only had Violet succeeded in making me look more grown up and sophisticated but, somehow, she managed to make me look more confident too, and all with a couple of strokes of the hairbrush.

'You're a genius,' I said to her gratefully.

'I hear the cars coming. We'll give them a few minutes, and then go down.'

I patted my powder puff over my nose, dabbed rouge on my cheeks, and ran my lipstick across my lips.

★ ★ ★

Downstairs, people were milling, greeting one another. Zak's friend, Fred, greeted me with, 'Nice to see ya, it's been a long time,' which was an improvement on the last time I'd met him.

'See, you needn't have worried,' Violet said as we went out into the garden. 'They're not that bad a bunch after all.'

'Zak knows a lot of people,' I said, looking at the girls frolicking around, laughing gaily.

'Socialites most of them, a shallow lot, never out of the limelight,' Violet said dismissively.

Zak appeared, resplendent in tuxedo and bow tie. As soon as he saw us he came straight over.

'Violet, Ellie, how are you doing? So good of you to come,' he said, pleased to see us.

'It's great to be here,' I said, meaning it as I looked into his eyes.

He beckoned a waitress with a drinks tray, and I took a glass of something frothy, with a hint of lemon and lime, it tasted delicious.

'This is real good,' I said, feeling lighter, as if the burden had been lifted. 'Happy birthday, Zak,' I said, raising my glass.

'And here's to many more,' Violet joined in, toasting him good health too.

At that very moment I spotted Gloria. In a short black frock, her long legs encased in flimsy stockings, she was more alluring than ever. When she saw me her eyebrows arched above her startled eyes. 'Just look at who it is, Zak's little friend from the ship!' she exclaimed, looking me up and down with her astonished eyes.

Oh God! She was coming over, walking as if she owned the place. I felt like turning and running away, but with nowhere for me to flee I stood stiff with apprehension, wishing I could be swallowed up in the crowd.

'Hi,' she said, wiggling her fingers condescendingly. 'Ellie, isn't it? How did you fish an invitation?'

Violet, taken aback, said, 'Ellie's our *friend*.'

'But I thought you'd gone back to the bogs of Ireland.' Gloria's eyes were insulting.

'And I thought you were in England,' I managed to say without snarling.

'Yes, I was in London. I'm just back. Daddy insisted on me making the trip with him.' She turned to Violet. 'We met his old friend, Lady Bowes Lyons – the Queen Consort. Oh, you should see her, she's so beautiful.'

'Did you visit her at the palace?' a chinless young man asked in an amazed voice.

'Oh no . . . we met at the Ritz for tea. It was the best fun. My God, it's the most gorgeous place I've ever seen,' she said gaily.

'How swell!' exclaimed someone.

Gloria glanced around at her gathering audience. 'Zak would have loved the wild London parties I got invited to. They went on all night, and they had the best music. London is so different to Boston,' she went on, her bragging increasing my dislike for her.

Her eyes lit on Zak as he returned. 'Those were wonderful letters you wrote to me, Zak. You were brilliant to keep in touch. You must come and visit Mom and Dad,' she rushed on. 'They were only saying that they haven't seen you for the longest time.'

He nodded enthusiastically. 'You're right, I must go see them.'

She drew him aside. I couldn't take my eyes off of him as he bowed his handsome head courteously towards her, as if what she was saying to him was for his ears only. Then he threw back his head with a sparkling laugh that transformed his face.

She joined in, her tinkling laughter grating on my nerves. 'Oh, Zak, I do wish you'd stayed on in Washington. We had such fun there. Boston is so fusty and so is that old bank of yours.'

'But I like banking.'

'I know, honey, but you've got so much energy, and such great ideas. It's a shame not to use them. You know you could be an entrepreneur, or anything you wanted to be,' Gloria gushed, with an impatient gesture of her hand. It was obvious to me that it wasn't Zak's ambition that mattered to her but her own.

'Zak's getting bored, let's break them up,' Violet said, going forward, calling to the waiter holding a tray of long-stemmed frosted glasses. 'Have you tried any of the other fruit cocktails, Gloria?'

'I don't believe so,' Gloria simpered. She gave Violet a sweet smile as she reached for a glass, while I helped myself to another lemon cocktail.

I regarded Gloria's close-set eyes, her upturned, disdainful nose, and her narrow mouth, wanting to smack her right between the eyes.

'She's silly and spoilt. Don't let her get to you, that's what she wants,' Violet said under her breath, and we moved off.

Out of the corner of my eye I saw Zak's mother, a vision in a glittering gold dress, drifting towards us. Oh God, what would I say to her?

'Violet! Great to see you here! You're looking wonderful,' she said, hugging her.

'You remember Ellie, don't you?' Violet said.

Mrs Rubens turned to me and gave me one of her social smiles. 'Ah, yes, I do.' She stood an uncomfortable distance from me. Arching her eyebrows quizzically, she said, 'I didn't know you were still around . . . What have you been up to?'

I told her about my new hat store.

'How smart of you,' she said with a false brightness. 'Let's hope you stick at it.'

'Once I start something I have to see it through. I never let go of anything,' I said enthusiastically.

'So I've noticed.' Mrs Rubens glanced meaningfully

towards Zak, who was making his way over to us.

'Ellie makes the most wonderful hats. You should call in and see for yourself. You'll be sure to find something out of the ordinary,' Zak said as he joined us. 'There's a lot of potential in Ellie, she's going to do something exceptional one day.' His smile to his mother was boyish and challenging. 'She's from this new generation of women who seize the chance to do something for themselves.'

'Really!' Mrs Rubens said in surprise, looking me up and down. 'It seems Miss O'Rourke has a number of unexpected talents.' Her voice was heavy with condescension, as if she wanted to drag me down.

'She has.' Zak looked pleased by what he blindly took to be her approval of me.

Gloria, catching the undertow of her sarcasm, smiled delightedly, but said nothing.

The band arrived and set up. Among them was a large, immaculately-dressed black man, holding a trumpet aloft.

I nudged Violet. 'Violet, who is that man? He looks familiar.'

'It's Louis Armstrong!' she squealed. A cheer went up and, suddenly, swooning, laughing girls surrounded Louis.

'Zak!' Violet called him. 'You never told us!'

'It's a surprise,' he called back.

'Howdy!' Louis flashed a schoolboy smile at us, and

introduced his new band, the Hot Five. 'Now let's party,' he called out.

His face aglow, his eyes twinkling, he started with 'Chop Suey', which sent us into a frenzy of dancing. Everyone was on the floor. Beaming, trumpet flashing, he went on with his new hit, 'Heebie Jeebies', like a man possessed, his wife, Lil, ripping up and down the piano as she raced to keep up with him. After a while, exhausted, we stopped to take a breath as he carried on in his gravelly voice with 'Evening Star'. Then, joyously he started 'My Blue Heaven'. Thrilling quivers ran down my spine, making me almost want to cry with rapture. He caught my eye and gave me a wicked smile that made me forget everything. Louis Armstrong and his band, they were infectious, revolutionary. He was untouchable, and we were hooked.

Supper was served late. Zak whisked Louis and the band into the house for a private meal while the rest of us were treated to a buffet served from a table that ran the length of the tent. Violet gazed at the mountains of delicious food murmuring, 'Oh, I can't eat a thing; I'm so in love with him.'

'So am I.'

I nibbled a cocktail sausage while she pecked daintily at an hors d'oeuvre, anxious for Louis and the band to return. As soon as they appeared we were out on to the dance floor again.

'Now, I'll really make you move,' said Louis in his

Southern drawl, sending us wild, clicking his fingers, tapping his toes. Dancing the Charleston we lost control, then the Cake Walk, and the Turkey Trot until we collapsed in a heap laughing.

'This is wonderful,' I said, the songs thrumming in my brain.

Suddenly Zak was beside me. 'It's the Black Bottom. Won't you dance?' He grinned, taking my hand.

'I don't know it.'

'I'll show you, it's like nothing you've seen before,' he said, stretching out his hand to me, and he spun me round, easy in his movements, not caring who was watching.

'Exciting, isn't it?' he said above the music.

I nodded, but stumbled on the last spin. Zak caught me. 'Are you OK?' he asked, his eyes veiled as he held me in his arms.

'I'm fine,' I laughed, feeling foolish.

As soon as it was over, Gloria grabbed Zak for the next dance. I made my way across the room, slipping through the crowd and out into the garden to cool down, and walked straight into Mrs Rubens. 'Ah there you are, Ellie. Enjoying the party?'

'It's sensational, and Louis is sensational. What a wonderful surprise.'

'I'm glad you're enjoying yourself.'

'Thank you.'

'I must say it was a surprise to see you here. Isn't it

wonderful to see Zak and Gloria becoming close again?' I felt a sudden dread overcome me. 'I expect they'll be announcing their engagement soon,' she added.

Everything went blank. My legs turned to jelly as I went to walk away. I closed my eyes to steady myself. Nothing had prepared me for the shock of hearing this. It wasn't true, it couldn't be. I found that I was struggling to keep calm. Mrs Rubens didn't seem to notice. 'She's wonderful, Gloria, perfect for Zak,' she ploughed on. 'They've known one another for ever – used to go everywhere together when they were kids. Oh, they fought at times. Zak hated her at one point, but that's all changed now. You can see that she'll do him a lot of good, can't you?'

I was imagining them standing next to one another, walking down the aisle of the little church that Zak and I were supposed to get married in, Louis Armstrong's band striking up as they entered a fabulous white tent.

'Now, let's keep it our little secret for the present. The reason I'm telling you now is because I don't want to see you get hurt.' She patted my arm and swayed off down the beach, her thin gold sandals sinking into the sand.

It was a beautiful night, a full moon hung in a cloudless sky, stars dotted around it, the sea beneath it dark velvet, a golden path reflected on it. I stood against the railings, drinking it all in, telling myself that I had nothing to fear from Zak's mom. She was a sad, lonely woman with little to do but interfere in her son's life.

Still, the tears fell unchecked as I realised that I had no rights over Zak. I wasn't even dating him. My eyes burned as I looked out over Hyannis Port to stop myself from asking him about Gloria. Gazing down at the boats in the harbour I felt suspended above them, like a bird. I wished I was a bird, and that I could fly out over the bay, leave everything behind.

'Ellie!' It was Zak. 'Are you OK, honey?'

I recovered myself quickly, determined not to let him see my devastation. 'I'm fine, it's just the effect Louis Armstrong has on me.' I smiled.

'I saw Mom talking to you. What's she been saying?'

I had to fight off the urge to confront him about what his mother had told me because I didn't want a row. 'We were chatting. She's surprised to see me here.'

'Typical Mom,' he smiled, embarrassed. 'She feels she has to keep tabs on me. Don't let her bother you.'

'She doesn't want me around.'

'It's not her business.' His eyes looked gravely into mine as 'Bye Bye Pretty Baby' played out over the air.

'Come on, let's dance,' he said brightly. 'They'll be wrapping up soon.'

I looked up at him. His face swam in front of my eyes as I thought, this is probably the last dance we'll have together, he and I.

Faint from Mrs Rubens's revelations, I went into his arms, closed my eyes and listened to the moan of the saxophone and the broken, jerky rhythms of the other instruments. For a blissful few moments, I forgot all about Gloria, and imagined that Zak was mine. As the song ended Zak held me tight. I wanted to tell him what his mother had said, and for him to reassure me that everything was going to be all right. But instead, reluctantly, I pulled away from him to see Gloria waiting in the wings, her obvious desire to have him all to herself evident. How foolish I was to imagine that I could ever have had a chance with him. I'd been wishing for something that would never be, I realised, as I excused myself and went in search of Violet.

'You look as if you've seen a ghost. Is something up?' she asked.

'Can we talk?'

'We can slip away when Louis and the band have packed up.'

I told her what Zak's mother had said. 'Well I never heard anything about an engagement,' Violet said in surprise. 'And surely Zak would have mentioned it to me.'

That night I fell into bed and mercifully went quickly to sleep. I awoke in the morning with a pounding headache and an ache in my chest. Violet was already up and dressed. I washed and dressed myself, and then went to find her in the kitchen, where she was making us a pot of strong coffee.

'Morning, Ellie. Want some coffee? . . . Zak and I went for a swim.'

'Where's Gloria?'

'She's still asleep.'

Zak came in, a big towel over his shoulders. 'You should have been up earlier. The water's warm.'

'I slept it out.'

'Good party, eh?'

'Sensational,' Violet said.

'Are you coming to see the Red Sox play this afternoon?'

'No, we've got to get back to Boston. I promised Dora I'd be there this afternoon when it gets busy.'

'Sure, I'll see you back there then.'

He was gone, whistling a ragtime tune, not a care in the world.

Thirteen

Dora was flicking through a copy of *Vogue* when I arrived back at the shop.

'Not rushed off your feet?' I asked, disappointed.

'Just done the last orders,' she sighed. 'But tell me about the party? Was it very glamorous?'

I filled her in, leaving out any mention of Zak, but my heart felt heavy. I kept thinking about him. How he was so brilliant and charming, and more than anything he was comfortable in his own skin, and he made people feel at ease in his company. I could see, for the first time, that there had never been any serious possibility of us spending the rest of our lives together. I was too young, too vulnerable; but more than that, Zak could never understand how very important my dreams of success were to me. And, above all else was the fact that had always been there, staring me in the face. I realised that Gloria was perfect for him. She had the right background, and she was beautiful too.

That night I sat down and wrote to Zak, telling him that I thought it would be better for us not to meet socially again, and wishing him every happiness with Gloria.

But the telegram that arrived the next morning wiped all despair over Zak out of my mind.

Alice has gone missing. Please inform us if she is with you.
Uncle Jack

I clutched it against my chest, as the room began to spin around me.

'What's up?' Dora asked.

I looked at her, and felt as if my heart had cracked and broken apart. 'Alice has run away. What if something dreadful has happened to her?' I burst into tears.

'Oh no!' Dora came to me. 'Shh, don't cry,' she said, putting her arms around me. 'She'll show up, honey, she's probably on her way here this very minute.'

'But what if she doesn't?'

'Maybe she'll have taken herself off for a jaunt somewhere, and you'll hear from her.'

'I should have brought her back with me when I saw her in New York.' The tears ran down my cheeks.

'Hush now, she'll turn up and be just fine, you'll see.'

No matter what Dora said I was twisted with anxiety. Alice had gone like she'd threatened, and I was to blame. I'd neglected her, let her down by reneging on my promise to bring her to Boston and take care of her. All our wonderful plans for the future had come to nothing in her eyes. As far as she was concerned I'd betrayed her by abandoning her, and this was my punishment.

I paced the room, wringing my hands in anguish, not knowing what to do.

Dora phoned Violet, who came as quickly as she could. She read the telegram. 'She went missing yesterday. Supposing she's on her way here, and got held up for some reason?' Violet said.

'I'm not hanging around waiting to find out. I'm going to New York.' I looked at Dora, expecting her to give me one of her disapproving looks. Instead she glanced at the clock and said, 'If you get goin' now you'll catch the 10.30 train.'

Violet said, 'Do you want me to come with you?'

'No, thank you . . . I'd better go alone. This could take time.'

Dora said, 'I'll take care of everything, let you know if she arrives meantime.'

'Thanks, Dora.'

Violet said, 'Take sensible shoes, I expect you'll be doing a lot of walking.'

I rushed around gathering a few necessities for the journey, and Violet had me at the station in the nick of time.

As the train came in, Violet put her arms around me. 'You'll find her,' she assured me, seeing my doubtful expression.

'And I'll scold her severely when I do.'

'That's better,' she smiled. 'Now if you need me to come to New York just holler. Promise me.'

I promised I would, and begged her not to tell Zak what had happened. 'I need to deal with this myself, it'll give me time to think.'

'What'll I say when he asks where you are?'

'Tell him Aunt Sally's ill, and I've gone to see her.'

On the journey my anxiety washed over me in waves as I wondered what could have happened for Alice to do such a drastic thing. OK, she was unhappy, but she had always been an optimistic girl – always looking on the bright side. Had Mary-Pat gone too far with her bullying? Had Uncle Jack frightened her in some way?

The train racketed along, the wheels howling on the tracks, me howling inside. As I gazed out the window at the vast expanse of sky I thought of her being on her own, without protection. Anything could happen to her. I realised, for the first time, what it must have been like for her when I'd run away from Uncle Jack's the previous year, and I felt deeply sorry for the pain I must have caused her. More than ever I was determined to find her. I would hug her and apologise to her for abandoning her, and I'd scold her for the agony she'd put me through.

As soon as we arrived in Brooklyn I sidled up the narrow passage clutching my suitcase, impatient to get off. Out on the sidewalk I hailed a yellow cab to Uncle Jack's.

Aunt Sally looked shrunken and haunted when she answered the door. 'Oh, it's you, Ellie!' she said, unsurprised.

'I came as soon as I could.'

She ushered me inside, saying, 'I don't want to talk to any of the neighbours right now. The whole neighbourhood's aware of what's happened. Oh, the shame of it!' She dabbed her red eyes with a handkerchief.

Everything about that miserable house was exactly the same, except that Alice wasn't there to greet me with her quick smile and her high, delightful laugh.

Watching her, I felt detached. 'How long has Alice been gone exactly?' I asked.

'Since yesterday evening.'

I followed her into the family room, where a subdued Mary-Pat was sitting with her arms across her chest in a guarded pose.

'Hi, Ellie,' was all she said.

Aunt Sally said, 'Alice didn't come home from her Irish dancing lesson, did she, Mary-Pat?'

'She didn't even show up at the class,' Mary-Pat said, as if to stop herself from getting the blame, but obviously worried by it all.

'When she still wasn't back we searched the house, the yard, even the shed where she hides out sometimes. We asked the lodgers if they'd seen her. They hadn't. Mrs

Fallen next door remembered seeing her waiting for a trolley bus uptown and thought nothing of it. We thought she'd surely be back before night. Mary-Pat hung out the window all evening scanning the street for her, didn't you Mary-Pat?'

'Yeah,' Mary-Pat nodded. 'Yeah! See she's always taking herself off, and she talks to people she doesn't even know.'

Aunt Sally nodded. 'She'd chat to any passing stranger even though she's been warned not to, and as you know there's all sorts of riffraff around. We went and asked in all the stores where she's known. But nobody could recall seeing her. Then it was growing dark and the neighbours went down all the streets looking for her but couldn't find her,' she continued. 'I went down the list of names of girls in her class that Mary-Pat had given me, and phoned their homes. "Have you seen Alice?" I asked. None of them had. This morning I went down to the school with Mary-Pat and asked all the teachers, and they asked all the children. We spent all day going from one house to another, searching yards, and streets. Oh, it's all so awful.' A tear slid down her cheek.

'Did you call the police?'

'Yes, but they won't get involved until she's been missing a full twenty-four hours,' said my aunt.

Uncle Jack arrived. He took one look at me and said accusingly, 'I can't understand it, she had a good home here, had everything she could want; only she didn't appreciate it. Just like you, she didn't know when she was well off.'

'Well, it's quite obvious that Alice was an outsider here, just as I was.' A silence fell at this shocking remark. 'Well, it's true, isn't it?' I looked at him. He flinched but said nothing.

'Why can't you be nice for once?' Aunt Sally said to me, and went into the family room and poured herself a stiff gin and tonic.

I escaped down to the kitchen. Bridget was dry-eyed but pale as an eggshell.

'Oh, Ellie, it's terrible about Alice,' she said, getting to her feet, putting her arms around me.

We sat down together. 'Bridget, what really happened?' I asked her.

She shook her head slowly. 'I don't know very much, only that Alice has changed in the last while. She became quite difficult, so unlike her. She was never satisfied with anything, and she was always wandering off. It was obvious that she wasn't happy. And lately she thought that anywhere would be better than living here.'

'Did she tell you this?'

'Oh yes, often.' She began to cry. 'It's my entire fault. If it hadn't been for me she might be here still. Oh, why I said anything I don't know.'

I took her hand in mine. 'Bridget, how is it your fault? Tell me!'

Calming herself, she said, 'Well, one day, a short while

ago, she confided in me that this boy had invited her to the cinema. I told her not to go, and not to speak of it to her aunt or there'd be trouble. I cautioned her about going out with strange young lads, but she argued with me – said she knew him and that he was a nice chap. I quizzed her about him but she wouldn't tell me anything. I told her that she was too young to date, and that wasn't the way she'd been brought up. Oh, the poor, poor girl,' she sobbed.

'What did Alice say to all that?'

'She just listened to me, or she seemed to. Anyway, the next day she came home late and I accused her of being with this boy and she lost her temper with me. She said, "I'm not staying here, nobody wants me." And she looked so heartbroken. I felt sorry for her. I made her a cup of hot chocolate and told her that she had it all wrong.'

'What about this boy? Who is he?'

She shrugged helplessly. 'I don't know who he is, or where she knows him from. She wouldn't say.' Her voice trembled. 'You see Alice never thought she was doing anything wrong, she just wanted to be out all the time, and that was that. Oh, I'll never forgive myself if anything happens to her. I can't bear not knowing where she is,' she sobbed hopelessly.

'Don't cry, Bridget, we'll find her,' I said, trying to comfort her, my own tears threatening. 'Did Aunt Sally upset her?'

'No, that's the problem, she didn't bother with her at all.' Bridget lowered her voice. 'Mary-Pat wasn't nice to her either. It wasn't right, the way she was treated.'

'Alice did tell me that Mary-Pat was horrible to her, but to be honest, I thought she was exaggerating. They got on so well when I lived here.'

Bridget nodded. 'She wasn't exaggerating, though I can't say more than that, I have to live here, and your aunt and uncle are people to be afraid of when something goes badly wrong.'

I heard the step on the stair. Bridget dried her eyes quickly on her apron, not wanting to be seen crying.

Aunt Sally came into the kitchen, as intimidating as ever, to enquire from Bridget what was for supper. Seeing that Bridget was upset she said, 'I don't know why you blame yourself, Bridget. I personally think Alice's hiding out, doing this for spite.'

'I'm sure there's an explanation,' I said, clenching my teeth together to stop myself from screaming at her. 'Is it all right if I go up to her room? Have a look around.'

'I suppose so,' she said stiffly.

My heart thumped as I ran up the stairs to the box room at the top of the house that Alice and I had shared. The blind was drawn, and it was full of shadows, and full of the smell of Alice. A half-eaten slice of toast and peanut butter lay on her bed beside her forlorn-looking teddy bear.

I opened every drawer of her chest of drawers, and

took out each item of clothing carefully. There were matchbooks, safety pins, and a jewellery box containing her Irish dancing medals in the bottom drawer, and an old pocket book hidden beneath a woollen scarf. I lifted it out, unzipped it and took out a comb, a bunch of candy wrappers, slides, clips, and a pack of playing cards.

I searched her wardrobe for the pocket book I'd sent her for Christmas but it was nowhere to be found, neither could I find her purse. There was no doubt in my mind that Alice had planned her escape – and it was time to take action. I ran back downstairs, told Aunt Sally of my discovery, and insisted that she ring the police immediately.

The patrol car arrived within ten minutes. Two serious-looking cops came into the house.

'I'm Sergeant Malone,' said the older one in a distinctly Irish accent.

Uncle Jack brought them into the family room, pulled out a chair each for them. Calmly Sergeant Malone asked how long Alice had been living here, where she'd come from, and all about her. Aunt Sally, her eyes fearful, replied to some questions. I answered others. The scratch of Sergeant Malone's pen across the pages of his notebook gave no indication as to what he was thinking. Finally he put away his notebook.

'Have you checked the hospitals?' he asked.

'Yes,' Aunt Sally murmured. 'Nothing.'

Then the lodgers were questioned one by one, but to

no avail. The last time any of them had seen Alice was at breakfast time the previous morning.

Sergeant Malone said, 'This sort of thing happens all of the time. Kids wander off from their homes for one reason or another, but most are reunited in the end. I'm sure you'll find she's gone off with one of her friends. Anyone else in her group missing?'

'Alice doesn't have any close friends at school,' Mary-Pat told him.

'Did she have any other friends?' he asked.

'She must have had because she came home late most days. I assumed she was hanging around with kids, chatting – you know what they're like,' Aunt Sally said.

'And did she say where she'd been on those occasions?'

'No,' said Aunt Sally.

He trained his sharp eyes on her. 'You didn't think to ask her?'

'No. I haven't been myself for a while back. Not since I lost my baby some years ago. I need a lot of rest.' She looked away, tears in her eyes.

'I see,' said Sergeant Malone, looking at her with sympathy.

For the first time ever I felt sorry for her, realising that she had never recovered from Mia's death.

The other cop said, 'Some kids do stay out until all hours roaming all over the place, and no one bothers about them. No one reports them missing unless . . .'

'Unless?' Uncle Jack asked.

'They've been in trouble. Is there something else you're not telling me?'

'No, there isn't. Alice is a happy-go-lucky girl, full of fun . . .' Aunt Sally's voice trailed off.

Sergeant Malone asked, 'Has she been out of sorts lately?'

'No.' Aunt Sally was emphatic.

'But she was, Mom. When she was in she stayed in her room most of the time.'

'That's right, she did,' Bridget agreed.

'So, Alice was depressed,' he said matter-of-factly, taking out his notebook, jotting it down.

'No, she was bored,' Aunt Sally said firmly.

Sergeant Malone closed his notebook and stood up. 'I'd like to have a look in her room, if you'll show me where it is please.'

'You won't find anything, we've already looked,' Uncle Jack said.

'I'd still like to check it out anyhow,' he insisted.

Upstairs, he opened the musty wardrobe and gazed at her Irish dancing costume, and the taffeta skirt Aunt Mabel had sent her for her fifteenth birthday. He pulled out the drawers, one by one, emptied poor Alice's clothes out on to her bed and rummaged through her meagre possessions. Picked up her little gold address book, and flicked through the pages.

'You've checked with all of these people?'

'Yes,' Aunt Sally confirmed.

He put the address book in his pocket, looked around, then left the room abruptly, leaving the contents of Alice's chest of drawers scattered on her bed.

Downstairs, he said, 'We'll start the search immediately.'

'Thank you.' Aunt Sally opened the front door to see a group of neighbours standing around in the fading light, looking full of concern.

'Any news of Alice?' one of them asked.

'No, not yet,' Uncle Jack said gruffly, shutting the door in their faces.

The shock of Alice's disappearance, and fear of what might have happened to her, was relentless. We sat around the dinner table like figures frozen in time, silent except for the empty sound of cutlery scraping on plates. I wanted to flee from the house, and all of them, but I had no choice but to stay until the bitter end. As soon as the meal was over I heaped the uneaten food into a dish, piled up the empty dishes, and took them downstairs, where I helped Bridget to do the wash up.

The sharp pain of sadness was etched on Bridget's face. Each time she glanced at the clock she seemed to be losing hope of Alice returning, though she didn't say so. I couldn't think of anything to say to comfort and reassure because my own expectations were fading.

Finally, she took herself off to bed, and I waited by the phone in the hope that it would ring – but it didn't.

In desperation I lifted the receiver to dial the number of the police station, and replaced it knowing that they would contact us if there were any news.

Eventually I went up to her room, and replaced her things carefully in the drawers and the wardrobe.

The sparseness of the room reminded me of the first day we'd arrived here, the cold reception from Aunt Sally, and Alice's terrible homesickness.

I looked out of the window across the rows of chimneystacks and rooftops to the sky, convincing myself that Alice was out there, somewhere, and that I was going to find her. Snatches of songs floated up from a radio, and the final call of a settling bird made me painfully aware of the strangeness of the house without her.

Finally, I got into Alice's bed, covered myself with her grey blanket, rested my head on her worn pillowcase, longing for it to be just like it had been before; both of us lonely, yet each of us a comfort to the other.

I stayed awake for a long time in faint hope of hearing a knock on the door, and footsteps rushing upstairs, and Alice's voice greeting me. But there was no knock – there was nothing but silence. It spread up from the kitchen, over the whole house like a spell. It even spread out on to the street, and the whole area.

In that terrible silence I thought of how Alice had

cried when I told her I couldn't afford to take her with me to Boston, and how she hadn't understood when I tried to explain the difficult financial situation I was in. Now I wished with all my heart that I'd thrown caution to the wind, packed up her things, and taken her away with me there and then. I sank down into the bed and wept.

Eventually, I fell asleep and dreamed that Alice and I were back home in Ireland, swimming in the sea, ducking one another, then diving off the rocks, Alice breaking the surface first calling out, 'Ellie, where are you?'

I woke with a start, thinking that I'd really heard her voice calling me. But there was no one there. Exhausted, I lay breathless, afraid of the day ahead.

Fourteen

Next morning I got out of bed, tiptoed to the window and pulled the blind.

Everywhere was still. The morning was mercifully cooler. Downstairs, the whole place was in darkness, the blinds pulled down. It was as if the house was grieving too, and was sunk in a dreadful gloom.

Bridget, bleary-eyed from lack of sleep, came into the kitchen and padded about preparing breakfast.

'Did you sleep?' she enquired.

'On and off. I was thinking about Alice. My biggest fear was that she'd set out for Boston and had been kidnapped on the way.'

'I kept thinking of her, out all night on her own, maybe lost in the dark some place.' Her chill words held the threat of something unbearable. 'May God protect her, and guide us in the right direction,' she said, blessing herself, and raising her eyes heavenward. The light from the window cast a pale sheen on her skin.

The sound of the lodgers rising broke our desolate

thoughts. Busily, I set the table and put the coffee on while Bridget poached eggs.

'I'm going to the police station,' I said, swallowing a mouthful of coffee and heading out the door, unable to wait a minute longer to hear news of Alice.

The waiting room in Brooklyn Police Station was plastered with posters of missing people, and of wanted men with numbers on their heads. I explained who I was to the cop on duty. He lifted the phone and spoke to someone. I sat on a chair, waiting for Sergeant Malone to come out of his office, dreading what I might be told.

Eventually I was called into Sergeant Malone's office.

'Good morning, Miss O'Rourke. Still no sign of your sister, I'm afraid,' he said gravely. Taking out a file from a filing cabinet, he removed a foolscap page of typing and passed it to me. 'This is the report we've compiled on her,' he said, handing it to me.

As I read through it, the words *nervous debility* jumped out at me.

'This is wrong, Alice didn't suffer from nervous debility,' I told him.

'Perhaps not but my hunch is that she took off because she was feeling low at the time. That's the most likely scene,' he said.

'Took off to where though?'

He shrugged. 'Could be anywhere just to get

attention, happens all the time.' The look on his face made me think that this was routine to him and that he wasn't all that concerned about Alice. Or maybe he was trying not to panic me?

I knew in my heart of hearts that there had to be a more plausible reason for her leaving than that, and I didn't believe that she'd return of her own free will either.

'I don't believe this theory, and I'm not letting her get filed away under "missing persons" either, and forgotten about.' I swallowed hard to keep back the tears.

'That won't happen, Miss O'Rourke, I can assure you.'

'I'm scared that she's lost somewhere . . . and . . .'

'Try not to speculate. We're doing our best to find her.' From his look I sensed that he already had a plan of action.

'Thank you.' I threw him a grateful glance, satisfied that he would do his best.

Carefully choosing his words, he said, 'First off, we're sending out a radio appeal, asking if anyone has seen her. And we're putting posters up locally; in the shopping precinct, the subway and bus station. I'll need a recent photograph of Alice and I'll need you to find out what she was wearing when she left home.'

'I'm sure there is a recent photograph somewhere,' I said, relieved that something positive was being done.

'And since last evening, we've been doing a full search

of every nook and cranny of Brooklyn. Now tell me, why did you and your sister come over from Ireland? Was it to get away from the Troubles?'

'No, Alice and I came here first of all to get an education – the chance of a better life. You see, my father drowned so we had to leave our farm . . .' I couldn't hold the tears back any longer.

'I'm sorry to hear that. It must have had a terrible effect on you both.'

'Yes, at the time it did, not that we talked about it much. It didn't help to keep going over it.'

He nodded. 'I understand.' Seeing me to the door, he said, 'Try not to worry too much about Alice. I'm sure we'll find her for you.' He gave my shoulder a reassuring squeeze as he saw me out.

Aunt Sally was in the kitchen having a cup of coffee with Mary-Pat and Bridget when I got back to the house. I showed them the copy of the report.

'How dare they write down that Alice suffered from nervous debility for all the world to see. That's a state of mental illness,' Aunt Sally fumed.

I told them about the SOS that would be transmitted on all of the news bulletins. 'The police want a recent photograph of her,' I said.

'I'll get one.' Mary-Pat jumped up at once and went off.

She returned with a photograph of Alice taken at the

finals of an Irish dancing competition; Alice in her green-and-cream costume, her hair a mass of ringlets, her medal pinned on her chest, was smiling proudly.

'Sergeant Malone wants to know what she was wearing when she left.'

'I've no idea,' said Aunt Sally, mystified.

'Her blue gingham summer frock isn't in her wardrobe,' Mary-Pat said.

'She might have taken her white cardigan with her,' Bridget said.

I returned to the police station with Alice's photograph and gave them the description of what she was wearing. Then, at ten o'clock we huddled around the Bakelite radio to hear the news.

'*Radio Brooklyn,*' the announcer said in a Yankee drawl. '*Police at Brooklyn Police Station are appealing for any information about a missing girl. Fourteen-year-old Alice O'Rourke has been missing from her home, Number 21, Beech Street, Brooklyn, for over twenty-four hours. Police are growing increasingly concerned. Alice O'Rourke left her home the morning before yesterday and has not been seen since. We're anxious for members of the public to report any sighting of Alice or to give us any information they think might be helpful, however little it may be. If you think you've seen her please get in touch with us without delay.*

'*The missing girl is about five foot one, slim with mid-length curly blonde hair. She was wearing a blue cotton sundress and white plimsolls. Police are anxious to hear from anyone who may have seen a young girl fitting her description on or in the area of the docks. If you have any information at all, please telephone.'*

I sat gazing at the radio, hoping that Alice might hear this and come back, walk in the door, laugh off the fuss that was being made over her disappearance.

Mary-Pat's chest heaved. 'Maybe she's fallen into a hole, and is gone for ever. Oh, I wish I'd been more of a pal to her,' she sobbed.

'Well, no use crying about it now.' Bridget gave her a bitter look.

'If she comes back I'll tell her that I'm sorry,' vowed Mary-Pat.

Their bleak chatter washed over me. 'I'm going out to start searching for her now,' I said.

'But where?' asked Aunt Sally.

'Anywhere . . . Do you want to come, Mary-Pat, show me the places she frequented?'

'Sure. I'll get my jacket,' she said, glad to be useful.

'And get me another photograph of her to bring with us.'

We spent the morning searching Prospect Park, and then going around the Botanical Gardens. In Brooklyn Heights we pounded the streets, went into Macy's and the other shops along Fulton making enquiries and showing Alice's photograph.

We went to the deli on Cobble Hill where Alice had

often bought a snack, then on to Carroll Gardens and other waterside neighbourhoods. In Williamsburg we searched through the shops and asked in the ice-cream parlours, which were just opening up for the day, if anyone had seen her. With no luck we sat on a bench to rest but soon we were off again, trailing around, ending up at Brighton Beach.

Along the boardwalk teeming with parents and vendors we searched each face. The smell of hot dogs made us hungry, so we bought one each and sat on a bench to eat them amid the cries of children and the sound of an accordion.

'There she is!' Mary-Pat cried, pointing to a girl in a blue gingham frock, facing the sea. The two of us raced forward to have a look, but it wasn't Alice.

We continued our search, popping into shops and peering through windows on the way, explaining to café owners and enquiring at amusement arcades, showing Alice's photograph to anyone we saw. At the end of the boardwalk a crowd was gathered to watch the boats. We scanned it for a hint of blue frock, and a mop of burnished curls.

'Now what are we supposed to do?' Mary-Pat asked anxiously.

'I wish I knew. Let's sit down for a bit.'

We sat on a bench to rest. Mary-Pat stared across the blue expanse of bay. 'What if Alice had leaned out too far over the rail and fell in?' Mary-Pat asked miserably.

'Don't say that . . . She'll be OK,' I said, unconvincingly. But for the first time since Alice's disappearance I felt sorry for Mary-Pat.

We took a trolley bus to the library. The librarian was at the desk checking books. 'I know Alice well, she comes in often, sits over there,' she said, her eyes swivelling around to the back bookshelf. 'Haven't seen her in a couple of days, I guess.'

In the church we asked Father Griffin, the parish priest. He said he knew Alice, and promised to pray to Saint Anthony for her safe return home.

'Is there anyone she used to meet with after school?' I asked Mary-Pat as we headed back.

'No.' Her face was ash-grey with tiredness.

'Think, Mary-Pat. Is there someone you've forgotten about? What about her Irish dancing class?'

'She has a friend, Kate, there. She doesn't have a telephone, but I know where she lives.' Though Mary-Pat was tired there wasn't a word of complaint from her as we walked the two blocks to Kate Sander's apartment in a dark building with a revolving door. We took a creaking elevator to the fourth floor apartment. A bolt slid back and a face peered out.

'Mrs Sander?'

'Yes, what is it?'

'My name is Eleanor O'Rourke. I'm Alice O'Rourke's sister, and this is my cousin, Mary-Pat.'

She opened the door further. 'I heard on the news

that she'd gone missing. What a shock!'

'Yes. I was wondering if your daughter, Kate, might know where she went to?' I asked, hoping against hope that Kate might be able to help us.

She stood back to let us in. 'Kate!' she called down the hallway.

A pretty girl of about Alice's age appeared, said 'Hi' to Mary-Pat.

'Kate, this is Alice's sister, Eleanor.'

Kate nodded nervously. 'I saw her a few days ago,' she said.

'Did she say anything about going away?'

'No, not that I can recall.' Alarmed, she said in a low voice, 'I don't know where she is, but she did say that she'd given up waiting for her sister to come for her.'

'When was that?'

'When we were riding the subway – last time I saw her.'

'Did she say anything else?' I asked.

She bit her lip, and looked nervously at her mother.

'This is important, honey. You must tell Eleanor if Alice was planning to run away.'

'She did say that she likes going places, and that she was going to go somewhere far away someday soon. She often rides the subway in the afternoons when she's bored.'

'Where to?'

'Queens, Central Park, it all depended on the mood

she was in.' She turned to her mother, her lip trembling. 'It's all I know.'

'That's OK, honey.' Mrs Sander straightened up and clutched her daughter to her. 'I'm so very sorry that we can't help you, I wish we could. Can I give you a cup of coffee?'

'No thank you, we've got to keep going.' Turning to Kate I said, 'Thank you for your help. If you hear anything, will you please let us know?'

'Of course we'll let you know,' her mother said, taking down Uncle Jack's phone number.

'I do hope you find her,' she said as we parted.

'We'll find her,' I said, more to reassure myself than her.

Mary-Pat and I went to the subway at Prospect Park, and showed Alice's photograph to the man at the ticket office. He looked down at it, and shook his head regretfully. 'I can't say that I sold her a ticket. Don't recall a girl on her own.'

We sat on a wooden bench next to grimy men who were idly watching the trains come and go. Mary-Pat's shoulders were hunched. There were lines of fatigue under her eyes and a look of defeat on her face.

'You can go back home if you like,' I offered, suddenly ashamed of my lack of consideration for her.

'I'm all right, I want to stay, it makes me feel as if I'm doing something to help. I'll never forgive myself if anything bad happens to her,' she faltered, pulling out her handkerchief, blowing her nose.

'Nothing bad will happen to her. She can't have vanished without trace,' I mumbled unconvincingly, as I looked at people gathering on the platform.

A train came into the station, the carriages shuddering to a halt; I looked up with a start to see Alice's face framed in the window. I brushed a hand across my eyes, unable to believe that it was her. But there she was, her hair tangled, her face pale as she waited to alight. Leaping to my feet, my heart soaring, I cried, 'Look, Mary-Pat, it's Alice,' pointing to the window of the train, and running forward calling 'Alice,' the scrape of wheels on the track drowning out my voice. I pushed my way forward to meet her as she stepped into the queue for the door, but the doorway was filled with people getting off, and the emerging crowd squeezed me on all sides and she was lost from view.

'Alice!' I screamed, looking around in panic.

'There she is!' Mary-Pat pointed to a girl pushing her way up the escalator, her head up, and her arms tight against her body.

'Alice!' The whistle blew and the train belched and screeched out of the station.

I shouldered my way up the escalator, bumping into other passengers, Mary-Pat at my heels.

'Hey, watch it!' someone shouted after me as I stumbled over the last step and lost her again. We made our way to the exit and stood examining everyone who was waiting for a streetcar, but she wasn't there. We went back into the station and watched a train rocking off into the distance, wondering if she was on it.

Had it really been Alice who had been swallowed up in that crowd, or had I imagined it?

'I'm not sure it was her ... I didn't get a proper look at her face,' Mary-Pat said, as though reading my thoughts.

It was the loneliest moment of my life.

Fifteen

The next morning, Alice's photograph was on the front page of the *Brooklyn Daily Eagle*. This made her disappearance even more heartbreaking. Fear and sorrow hung over the house like a mist. It was in the strangeness of the atmosphere, and in the stoop of Uncle Jack's shoulders. It was in Aunt Sally's eyes, Bridget's tears, and Mary-Pat's bowed head.

Aunt Sally, gazing at the photograph, said croakily, 'She had her whole life ahead of her, and a good one at that.' Her mouth was a thin line of regret. She turned to me reproachfully. 'Of course you were a bad example to her. I never thought I'd have to live through this again.'

I felt uncomfortable, and went back upstairs and searched through her few things once more, hoping to find some clue that might have been missed. *Oh God, please send her back to me*, I prayed to her little Sacred Heart statue. *I promise that I'll take better care of her.*

Later, as I was about to leave for the police station, Sergeant Malone arrived.

'Hi, Sergeant Malone.' I held my breath as I let him in.

Aunt Sally came rushing downstairs. 'Any news, Sergeant?' she asked.

'There's nothing positive yet. I just thought I'd drop by to let you know that we'd had lots of calls in response to the radio appeal, and the photograph in today's newspaper, and we're following all of them up.'

'That's good,' she said.

'Have you ever heard of a girl by the name of Tammy, works at the ice-cream parlour on the corner of Atlantic Avenue?'

'No.'

'She phoned in, said she knows Alice.'

'Mary-Pat might know her.' She called to Mary-Pat to come downstairs.

'Do you know Tammy at the ice-cream parlour?'

Mary-Pat nodded. 'Alice knows her better than me,' she said vaguely.

Sergeant Malone said, 'Alice was in the ice-cream parlour a couple of days ago. Tammy talked to her.'

'Oh! What did Alice say?' I asked him.

'Nothing specific, but I have a hunch this girl might know a bit more about Alice than she's letting on. I think if you were to go and see it might jog her memory.'

'I'll go straight away, Sergeant,' I told him, seizing this lifeline, as I saw it, gratefully.

The possibilities of this snippet of information were like a breath of hope being blown into my face as I hurried down Atlantic Avenue towards the pale, bright sea.

I spotted the ice-cream parlour with its huge ice-cream cone sign and delicious posters of pastel-coloured ice-cream sundaes before I reached it. Inside was busy – ice-cream-stained tots sat with patient parents, and couples smooched at corner tables.

A group of sailors came in, eyeing the pretty girl with big brown eyes who was cleaning the counter.

'Hey, Tammy!' one of them called out as they took a seat by the window.

'Yeah?' She sashayed over to them, her order book and pencil poised, a big smile on her face. 'What's it to be today, boys?' They ordered chocolate ice-cream, cream sodas, peach melbas. She spoke in a hushed tone as if she was sharing a secret with them, then, giggling at some remark one of them made, she returned to the counter, their eyes following her.

I took the table with the best view of the docks and the people who were sitting on benches watching the boats, having a smoke.

Tammy came over to me. 'Hi! What can I get you?' she asked, handing me a menu.

I scanned the menu: *Special ice-creams: molasses, ginger snap, chocolate decadence, banana pudding, and pecan pie.* I chose a double decker that would last so that I wouldn't have to leave quickly. When she brought it to me, I asked her if she knew Alice O'Rourke.

She went pink. 'Who wants to know?' she said guardedly.

'I'm Eleanor O'Rourke, her sister.'

'Oh! That's OK,' she sighed with relief. 'Only I don't want any trouble, my pa'd kill me if he knew I'd been involved with the cops. He owns the place, he hates the cops.'

'There won't be any trouble. Can you tell me where Alice might have gone to?'

She shook her head. 'I've no idea, but I suspect she may have gone off with her boyfriend.'

'She has a boyfriend?' This was what I didn't want to hear.

'Yep.'

'Are you sure?'

'Sure, I'm sure,' she laughed. 'She's been in here with him a couple of times.'

'What does he look like?'

'He's tall, nice-looking guy, older than she is.' She leaned closer. 'There was something strange about him . . .'

'Like what?'

'Oh, I dunno. He looked kinda creepy or somethin'.'

'Creepy?'

'Yeah, the way he sorta looked at her made me nervous, y'know. Maybe it's just that he was so possessive of her. Not that he need worry. She's fallen for him big time. She told me last time she was here that she might go off with him. That he kept askin' her to.'

'Did she say where to?'

'Somewhere far away, she said. I told her not to be silly, that she'd be in trouble if she did. Jeez, I wasn't expectin' her to disappear like this.' She raised her eyes to heaven.

I pictured Alice and her boyfriend on a beach in some romantic place, and felt a sudden fury with her.

'Do you know his name?'

'No, as I said, I've only seen him a couple of times. Would you like a coffee on the house? You look as if you could do with one,' she asked kindly.

'Thanks, I'd love one.'

I watched her pour the strong black coffee in a mug. 'Just what the doctor ordered,' she said, and smiled.

When I took a sip of it I felt instantly refreshed.

She said, 'Try not to worry too much about Alice. She'll be back before you know it.'

'I hope you're right.'

'Why don't you hang round the docks for a while? I've often seen Alice waiting there for him on my way home. He might work there.'

'OK, I'll do that.' I finished my coffee.

'And try the subway station of the St George Hotel if that fails. I've seen Alice hangin' around there too.'

I thanked Tammy, left her a tip, and said I'd catch up with her later on.

'Sure thing!' she said, going off to serve more customers.

I followed Tammy's directions and walked past the backs of the shops and houses facing the sea, stopping every few yards to look up narrow lanes, hoping for a sight of Alice. Further along, seagulls lined the ledge of a big ship that sat in the harbour. A gust of hot wind ribbed the sea, and rattled chains against boats.

I passed boarded-up warehouses, and came upon a magical inlet with small craft docked on either side of it. In the full tide, the place was filled with the strong smell of fish.

The docks were noisy with the rumble of heavy cranes and clanking chainsaws of men working on a tanker. Cranes and forklifts lay dormant in a shipyard and, further on, a freighter lay rusting in the water. Along the trolley tracks were more factories and warehouses.

I reached a bridge, sat down on a bench among people waiting for a ship to dock, and watched tug boats sail slowly by in the distance, their smoke trailing behind them, the sea around them pale as a silken scarf. I couldn't think of anything except Alice and this boyfriend of hers. I imagined them together, walking along hand in hand, and wondered how she'd managed to stay out for such long stretches without being missed?

Obviously Aunt Sally had allowed her too much freedom, probably because she hadn't cared enough about her to make rules.

I wondered what would happen if I were lucky enough to find her. What would she say? I thought of all the things I wanted to say to her, and wondered how I'd be with her.

A ship came into view and moored in the harbour, seagulls tossing above it like paper kites. There was the rumble and dull clatter of chains with the action of loading and unloading, and the voices of the dockers calling to one another.

Sailors in white-and-blue uniforms with tattoos on their arms queued to alight. I wondered if perhaps Alice's boyfriend was a sailor, with cropped hair, and arms covered in tattoos like the young men on the ship. No, Tammy would have mentioned that.

A gradual cloak of mist gathered over the sea as the sun set to the left, highlighting the Statue of Liberty, and casting shadows on the steel cranes. Coils of wire ropes turned black under a violet sky. Lights reflected in the water, and stars came out, and there was still no sign of Alice. Slowly, I retraced my steps, the thought of the journey back without her was unbearable.

Downcast and weary, I made my way to the subway and hung around beneath the shelter, scrutinising the faces of people milling around. I stopped dead in my tracks because there was Alice, standing a distance away, her arms encircling the barrier railings as if she was holding on to them for dear life, her eyes scanning the faces of people coming towards her.

My hand flew to my mouth to stop myself from calling out to her. As the platform emptied, a look of desolation crossed her face. She pressed her lips together as if to stop herself from crying. I desperately wanted to run to her, envelop her in my arms, but remembering Sergeant Malone's warning not to approach her, I stepped back into the shadows and waited.

After a few minutes, a young man appeared out of nowhere and tapped her on the shoulder. Alice turned to him; joy in her face as she held his gaze. 'Ah, there you are,' she said in a scolding voice. 'You took your time.'

'Couldn't get away.' His voice sounded exasperated, but there was no mistaking the spark of excitement and a promise in their exchanged glances as they moved out of the station.

Eamon!

It was my cousin, Eamon!

No! It couldn't be! Eamon was away at college.

Weak at the knees, I prayed that I might be mistaken, though knowing that I wasn't. It was Eamon's face that I was looking straight into. I followed them up the road, trying to get a proper look at him, to make certain it was him. The breeze ruffled her hair and she swept it back with her fingers. As they stopped to cross the street he pulled her against him. She stretched an arm across his back, hugged him to her. At the corner he turned to kiss her. It was Eamon. There was no mistaking his narrow face and sharp features. I wanted to shout out to them to stop, wait! I wanted to slam my fist into Eamon's smug face, and drag her away from him.

Instead I took a deep breath to calm myself. I followed them up the street, incredulous at the drama that was unfolding before my eyes. The horrible Eamon had lured her away. They must have been meeting in secret for ages. But how had he enticed Alice away like this, and for what reason?

Stealthily, I padded along after them, keeping under the shadows of dense trees that leaned over the wall to my left.

At the end of the sidewalk the street narrowed, and a path curved between laurel and holly bushes. I turned left down a narrow footpath that led to some woods.

Weeds brushed my legs as, careful not to trip and make noise, I followed them into the dark and dense woods. The air was damp and mouldy, and silent except for the caw of crows and a sudden laugh from Alice.

Eventually, I found myself in a clearing. Before me was a dilapidated shack, its paint peeling, weeds growing up around it. Beyond it the woods rolled off into darkness.

Crouched behind a tree, I watched Eamon take a key out of his pocket and open the door. 'I thought we'd never get here,' Alice said, leaning against him, smiling.

'Couldn't wait to see me, huh?' he said with a laugh.

My stomach lurched as they both disappeared inside, closing the door firmly behind them. A light flicked on in a window.

I dropped down on to the grass, wondering what to do, sick at the thought of my sister alone with vile Eamon! A fierce dread rose up in me as I imagined her being wrestled to the ground by him, forced to do things against her will. Yet in my heart I knew that whatever it was that they would do together no force would take place. Alice had looked at him with open desire. Somehow he'd seduced her – how he'd managed it was beyond me.

Ever since we had first arrived in New York, Eamon had had the advantage over us both of being our educated cousin, Jack and Sally's son. He'd lorded it over me, intimidated me, too. What if he was now doing the same to Alice? But it struck me that this situation was made much worse and more dangerous by her compliance. She was so young. I pictured them stretched out together on a bed, with their heads together, not a care in the world for the family they'd left behind – and could stand the thought of it no longer.

Burning with anger and frustration, forgetting the police warning to keep a distance, I went up to the door of the shack and banged on it furiously, desperate to get Alice away from that evil boy.

A few moments later, the front door opened slightly

and Eamon stood there, a look of shock on his face when he saw that it was me standing there.

'What'd you want?' he hissed.

'I came for Alice,' I said.

He laughed as if I'd cracked the funniest joke ever. 'Alice!' He looked puzzled as if he'd never heard of her. 'What makes you think she's here?'

'I saw her come here with you.'

'You saw nothing of the kind, now go away and leave me alone.' Just as he was about to bang the door shut in my face, a shadow appeared behind him. Alice peeped out of the door.

'Ellie!' She looked astonished. 'How did you find us?' Puzzled, she looked at Eamon. 'I thought you said that nobody knew about this place.'

'They don't – she must have followed us.'

'Alice, I've been frantically searching for you. Tammy at the ice-cream parlour told me where I might find you. Everyone's worried about you: Uncle Jack and Aunt Sally, and Mary-Pat.'

'I heard the SOS announcement on the radio.'

'Then why didn't you get in touch?'

Eamon said, 'You'd better come in!' and stood back to let me pass.

Trembling, not sure of what to expect, I went inside.

The place was dim and shabby, and there was a smell of trapped stale air as if it had been shut up for a long time. Alice stood holding on to the back of a chair as if to steady herself. 'I'm not coming with you.' She raised her chin and looked at me squarely. 'I'm staying here with Eamon. I'm not going back to Uncle Jack's.'

'But Alice, you've got to come back . . .'

She put her hands across her chest in that defensive way of hers. 'No I don't, I love Eamon, and he's going to take care of me.'

'What?' Astounded, I looked from her to Eamon. 'That's right, we're in love,' he said, smiling smugly at me.

'But you can't be, you're cousins.'

'That makes no difference,' he snapped. 'Plenty of cousins fall in love.'

'See,' Alice said triumphantly. 'I don't need you, or Aunt Sally and Uncle Jack. I've got Eamon and he means more to me than anyone else in the whole world.'

'You can't be serious!'

'I am. We're going away tomorrow, on a boat.' She looked at him with love, already imagining their flight out into the world together, filled with joyful possibilities.

I thought I was hearing things. 'Where to?'

Alice shrugged. 'Anywhere. We're leaving in the morning. I'm going to get a job working as cabin crew, and then who knows, I'll get a proper job when we land—'

'Alice!' Eamon stopped her.

'What happens when Uncle Jack finds out that you've both gone off together? He'll freak out!'

'It won't make any difference to us, we'll be far away. Anyway, what do I care about Uncle Jack?'

'He'll come and get you both.'

'We'll be married by then, living in a different country,' Eamon said.

'You can't marry your cousin.'

'There's no law against it,' Eamon said.

'You're under age, Alice.'

'I have a birth certificate saying that I'm eighteen. Eamon faked it.'

'But you *can't* go away with him, Alice, you can't go.'

Eamon laughed at my distress. 'She'll be OK. I'll look out for her. I have it all planned. We're going to see the world together.'

Alice smiled determinedly. 'See, Eamon has it all worked out.'

'I bet he has,' I said bitterly, thinking how he'd deliberately taken his time, and waited patiently for the right opportunity to steal her away.

'You can't blame me for wanting to go, Ellie. I couldn't stand it the way I was being treated, like I was nothing, and Mary-Pat always acting like she was better than me.'

'What about school? What about your future?'

She gave me a scathing look. 'Like you really care what happens to me!'

'I *do* care. Oh, Alice! I have plans for you.'

'Like what?' Eamon asked sarcastically.

Ignoring him I said, 'I was going to send you to learn dress designing. You're so artistic.'

'Hah! I don't believe you! You never came back for me.' Tears flashed in her eyes. 'I waited and waited for you to show up.'

'You can see now that you're wasting your time,' Eamon said, folding his arms, gloating at me.

Alice said, 'I'm tired, I'm going to bed.'

I took her hand to stop her. It felt so soft, as delicate as a bird's, as I tried to pull her out towards the door. She stumbled. Eamon caught her and held her. She leaned against him. He gave me a possessive look as he said to me, 'Alice's going nowhere with you.'

Panicked, I grabbed hold of her arm, tried to pull her forward. 'Alice, come with me, I'm pleading with you.'

'No!' She shook my hand away. Her eyes fixed on me defiantly, and then she looked up at him for some clue as to what to do next.

Eamon said threateningly, 'You heard her, back off.'

I wanted to convince my sister that Eamon was no good for her, and that she was being held in a type of prison with him, but I knew it would be useless to even try.

'She'll be fine with me,' he said, giving me a sickly smile. 'We'll have a good time together, won't we, honey?'

'We sure will,' she smiled.

'Now you go to bed, get some rest, while I have a

little talk with Ellie, explain a few things to her.'

'OK,' she said, looking at Eamon. Then turning to me, she said, 'Bye, Ellie. I'll write to you.'

She left the room quietly, and there was nothing I could do. Had I lost Alice for good?

Sixteen

W'on't you sit down, make yourself at home?' Eamon mocked.

'I'm leaving,' I said, 'and Alice is coming with me.'

'Not yet, we have to talk about this. There's a couple of things you don't understand,' he said, biding his time.

'I don't understand any of it.'

'Well, let me explain. Here's the thing. You'll stay here. In the morning, when Alice and I are gone, you can leave.'

'No. We're leaving right now.'

'No you're not, and you'll regret it if you try.'

I jumped forward. 'I'm going to get the cops. They'll stop you. You've as good as abducted Alice – brainwashed her in some way. She's only—'

'What!' Suddenly I was flat against the wall, with his hand on my throat.

'Relax, Ellie. Let yourself go a little. It'll be much easier for you if you do.' His face was close to mine as he said, 'Now, are you going to do things my way or do I have to make you?'

'Get off me,' I hissed. 'You're a kidnapper and a criminal. When the cops get you they'll arrest you and throw you into jail.' Fighting for my breath, I tried to push him away. That's when I saw the small grey gun in his hand, the trigger covered by his index finger. Seeing my astonishment, he laughed then stood back as if he had all the time in the world.

'It's loaded. I could blow you away with this if I wanted to,' he said with a smile.

'Where in God's name did you get that from!' I gasped.

'Oh . . . I have a few friends . . . contacts here and there.' Eamon smiled maliciously. 'Now . . . be a good girl and lie down on the couch and go to sleep . . . I'll get you a blanket.'

He was gone for just a second. 'Here, make yourself comfortable. You don't mind if I keep you company?' He sat down on a frayed armchair, covered himself with a rug. 'Goodnight, sweet dreams.'

My heart was pounding. I needed time to think. Eamon was clearly mad, unhinged, and he seemed to be involved in some kind of dark world that I had only read about in the papers. I pulled the blanket over me and feigned sleep. What if Eamon and Alice did manage to get away, and I never saw her again? I thought of Alice in a couple of years' time, miserable, half starved in some shack in the middle of nowhere, a baby to try and bring up on welfare, Eamon having deserted her.

I lay motionless in the dark for hours, waiting for Eamon to fall asleep. Finally, I raised my head, sneaked a look at him. I could just make out his tousled head and the gun on the floor beside him. I shivered, thinking of the power that was in that harmless-looking piece of metal. If it was loaded like he said it was, he could blow me to kingdom come with a pull of the trigger. If I could only get my hands on it *I* would have the power, and I could sneak out of here without fear, and go to the police station.

Quietly, I eased myself off the sofa, crept across to his chair, and stood watching his chest rise and fall as he slept soundly. Gingerly, I reached out and lifted up the gun, then crept by him out of the room. I found another door – hoping it was where Alice was sleeping. But when I tried the handle it was locked. Alice had shut herself in. I'd have to go and get help – fast – come back for Alice with the police.

The front door creaked as I opened it slowly. For a heart-stopping second I waited, listening. There wasn't a sound.

Outside, everywhere was quiet. I ran across the grass into the woods, and made my way back the way I'd come.

Dawn broke over the docks. The pale light shimmered on the water, the inlets branching out from the harbour like silver arteries.

Suddenly, I heard running footsteps behind me.

I stumbled over a wall and crouched down, the gun clenched in my hand. The footsteps stopped a few yards from me. I heard Eamon curse under his breath. I crawled along the ground, edging away from him, trying to find an escape route. Beyond the grass was a steep drop to a patch of wasteland. My stomach churning, my hand that gripped the gun shaking, I slowly began to climb down it.

Then, from nowhere, a hand shot out from behind me and grabbed my shoulder. The gun fell to the ground. Eamon, taut as a tiger about to spring on his prey, stood before me. There was a loud snap as I stumbled backwards on a branch. For a split second I thought he'd shot me, and screamed. He lunged at me, his sweaty face huge above mine, his eyes scary.

'Thought you'd got away from me, didn't you?' he said, hauling me up. He pointed the gun in my face, his raging eyes piercing into mine. 'I could do a lot of damage with this.'

'Don't shoot! Please don't shoot!' I whimpered.

'Listen, you behave yourself, and do what I tell you and you'll be OK.'

He could blow me to bits now, I thought, and what would happen to Alice if he did? I braced myself, and let him take me by the arm. His grip on me was so tight as he hauled me along that I let out a gasp. 'You're hurting me.'

'That'll teach you not to try and be too smart.' He

thumped his fist into my shoulder to push me on. I fell forward, gasping. He hoisted me up, prodded me forward with the gun. Coughing, spluttering, my heart thumping, my ears buzzing, I walked in front of him, the gun nudging into my back, my lips clamped tight to stop myself from crying out in agony.

His fingers dug into my arm like needle-pricks as he pushed me on. Trembling all over, stiff and sore, I made up my mind that I'd have to be strong for Alice's sake and try to think of a way to get away from him.

The ravine was to my left – if only I could push him down it. How great it would be if he'd vanished from the face of the Earth. But he was too strong for me, unless . . . I had an idea – I stopped dead in my tracks, stuck out my foot. He tripped over it and fell forward with a crash. The gun slipped from his fingers. White with rage, and gasping, his hand grappled and groped, grasping for it. I kicked his hand away, grabbed the gun, and kicked him again as he struggled to get to his feet. 'Ouch! You bitch, I'll get you for this,' he moaned.

'Step back or I'll shoot,' I said, pointing it at him, trying to keep it level with both shaky hands.

'Don't!' He took a step backwards and slipped down the bank. Grasping, flailing, he slipped further down. I kept the gun pointed to his head as he groped and clutched at tufts of grass. I watched with horror as the bank gave way beneath him and he was sinking further down, clutching at the air. 'Help!' he cried, his head twisting to and fro as he desperately looked for something to grasp on to. All I could see was his hair and his eyes wide with terror. 'P-l-e-a-s-e h-e-l-p . . .' His words were swallowed up as he sank further and further down into the ravine.

A scream broke from him as he fell like a bird, and slipped out of sight. I stood there, numb, waiting for him to appear again, but he didn't. I waited, listening for a sound from him, but there was none, only the sigh of the wind through the trees. What if he was dead? That would mean that I'd killed him.

Scared, but with the gun held tightly in my hand, cautiously looking around every so often, in case he'd pop up again out of nowhere, I made my way downhill to the police station I'd seen the previous day. There was a main road and a few cars. I almost ran out in front of them, making the drivers swerve.

Eventually I fell into the police station, banged the steel and wire grid that enclosed the inner door, and stood panic-stricken, wondering how I'd explain why I'd killed Eamon. A big cop with a badge in his cap appeared. 'What can I do for you, Miss?'

'I think I've killed someone,' I spluttered.

'Come in and explain,' he said, eyeing my filthy, torn clothes.

'You have to come. Something terrible has happened.' In a shaky voice, I went on to tell the cop what happened. 'You'd better come quick,' I added, shaking from top to toe. 'I'm sure he's dead.' I began to sob.

The cop regarded me slowly, then he turned to call, 'Hey Mick, this poor kid's in trouble.' Another cop appeared. 'She thinks she's shot a guy who was holding her sister hostage.'

'And my sister's all alone,' I said, shivering.

'OK, calm down. Now where did this take place?' the other cop said.

I gave him directions. 'Let's go.' They took me out to the patrol car. We drove back to the ravine. I pointed out the spot where I'd last seen Eamon. The cop edged his way down the ravine, while the other cop kept his eyes on the shadowy trees. The only sign of the frightening scene that had taken place earlier was the uprooted tufts of grass, and a shirt button.

'Let's find this sister of yours,' the first cop said, looking at me doubtfully.

We roared up the lane. The two cops jumped out. One ran to the door, the other stood to one side, a gun at the ready.

Alice came running out. Startled at the sight of the cop, 'Oh no!' she screamed. Her eyes were wide with fear. 'What's happened?' She ran at me. 'Ellie, why are the cops here? Where's Eamon?' she cried, looking around wildly.

'He's gone, ran off,' I lied, gripped by a wave of panic.

I caught her as she collapsed against me. The police officer grabbed her. 'It's all right, I've got her.'

She clamped both hands over her mouth. 'No, I don't believe you. He wouldn't have gone without me.'

'Well, he did. Now put your clothes on, and let's get out of here,' the cop said.

'I'm not going without him,' she cried, clutching her nightdress.

'Come on, honey . . . We'll come back for your boyfriend,' the cop said more gently.

'Where is he really?' Alice snivelled as I helped her to get dressed.

'I don't know. Don't worry, we'll find him.' She half lifted her limp body into the car. I sat in beside her, my arm tightly around her crumpled-up body. It was torture watching her slumped in the back of the car, her face white as snow.

'Is she going to be OK?' I asked anxiously.

'Sure! She's scared that's all. We'll take her to a hospital, have her checked out.'

'You're going to be OK, you're with me now,' I said, holding her limp hand.

She knitted her brows together but kept her eyes closed, and didn't speak until we got to the Brooklyn Hospital.

'I want to go back, Eamon will be looking for me,' she said as a tall, competent doctor in a white coat examined her.

'Don't worry about that now,' he said, shining a beam of light from a tiny torch into her eyes, focusing on them before moving on to her nose and ears. Then he pressed his fingers on her forehead. 'Does that hurt?'

'No.' She turned away.

His steady dark eyes on her were uneasy as he listened to her heart. With a fixed gaze, and in a gentle voice, he asked her some more questions. She answered with a 'yes' or a 'no' then twisted away from him.

He asked me to leave so that he could examine her further, and pulled the curtains right round the bed as I went.

I sat quietly on a chair outside, hunched and scared, knowing that in that small cubicle the doctor would find out everything that had happened to Alice. Finally, the doctor emerged.

'Hi, my name is Tony Martin,' he said, shaking hands with us all. 'I gave Alice a thorough examination. Physically she seems fine.'

'That's good news.' I breathed a sigh of relief.

Aunt Sally and Uncle Jack arrived. Aunt Sally, though glad that Alice had been found, was overwrought about Eamon's involvement in her disappearance. 'I'm sure Eamon's intentions were strictly honourable. He was trying to help her,' said a deluded Aunt Sally.

'When can we take her home?' Uncle Jack asked, brusquely shutting her up.

Doctor Martin screwed up his face. 'I'm afraid you're going to have to be patient for a while. She's seems to be very traumatised.'

'Traumatised!' Aunt Sally spat out the word. 'I never heard the likes. We're the ones who are traumatised. I know exactly what happened,' she said to the doctor. 'She went and got our son, Eamon, into this mess intentionally. Playing on his sympathy, no doubt. It was an act of defiance against me and my husband, that's what it was. She always was a handful, that girl.'

Doctor Martin raised his hands. 'Please calm down. It looks like Alice has been through quite an ordeal. She must rest as much as possible, and we need to run some tests on her.'

'What kind of tests?' Uncle Jack asked suspiciously.

'First of all a pregnancy examination—'

'Pregnancy examination!' Aunt Sally cried, wringing her hands. 'That's ridiculous, my son wouldn't put a finger on her.'

'It's normal procedure in these circumstances, Mrs Casey,' the doctor explained. 'And, given her strange behaviour I've arranged for our psychiatrist, Doctor Carey, to see her tomorrow,' he said, matter-of-factly.

'Psychiatrist!' said a puzzled Uncle Jack.

'Yes, I suppose she does need her head examining running off like that without as much as a by-your-leave!' said Aunt Sally. 'I ask you, Doctor, what normal girl would do a thing like that?' She was bitterly twisting the story to make Alice out as the villain.

'I realise that you've all had a shock, but I don't think this is the time or place for this conversation. Alice is very ill and, as I've already said, it seems to me that she's not fully responsible for the situation she found herself in.' Doctor Martin looked at Aunt Sally as if he wasn't really expecting her to understand.

'Of course she's responsible. She's not a child. If you ask me, she's been reading too many romances,' Aunt Sally countered in a low, furious voice.

Doctor Martin said, 'We know very little about your son, and his involvement in all of this. We'll know more if and when he is found.'

'I hope they find him soon, so he can explain himself,' said an angry Uncle Jack.

Aunt Sally said, 'I don't know what we're going to do if this makes the local newspapers.'

I stayed silent, not knowing what to say.

Before we left I said goodbye to a drowsy Alice and promised her that I'd be back first thing the next morning. As soon as she saw Aunt Sally and Uncle Jack she turned away.

When as we got back to the house I went straight upstairs to avoid having to answer questions, undressed quickly and took a lukewarm shower. My whole body ached as I slipped between the sheets. Bridget brought me up a tray with a hot mug of coffee and a muffin, and sat with me while I relayed the whole story to her.

'To think that the poor little mite was with that freak,

Eamon, all the time, and we never suspected it,' she said in amazement.

'Oh Bridget, I thought I'd killed him.'

'I wouldn't have blamed you if you had,' she said.

That night I wrote to Aunt Mabel to tell her that Alice was ill in hospital and that I didn't know what to do because I wasn't sure what exactly was wrong with her. I asked her not to tell Mam until I did.

Seventeen

The next morning I went straight to the hospital. My footsteps echoed along the corridor to the clean, white waiting room. I sat there wondering what the tests on Alice would reveal, and braced myself for the worst possible news.

A middle-aged nurse bustled in. 'You can come see her now,' she smiled. Heels clicking rapidly, she led me down the bright hall.

Alice was in a bed at the end of a long, half-empty ward. She lay still and pale, her eyes closed.

'We gave her a sedative to help her sleep,' the nurse explained. 'She'll come round soon.'

Slowly Alice opened her eyes.

'All right?' the nurse asked her, touching her face.

'Where am I?'

'You're in hospital, dear.'

'What's the matter with me?' she asked me as soon as the nurse left.

'Never mind that now, how are you feeling?' I asked.

'Dizzy.' She clutched the sheet like a baby would

clutch a toy, and slipped further down in the bed, already falling asleep again.

I sat watching her as she breathed slow, fitful breaths, her pale skin almost transparent. This wasn't the Alice I'd known all my life, the sister I'd grown up with. This was a stranger in a white hospital gown, *Property of Hospital* written across it. I thought back to Alice at home, in Ireland, in the garden picking fruit, or sitting on the back step reading, Shep, our dog, quietly at her feet, and had to fight to hold back the tears.

Eventually she woke up again.

'Feel better now?' I asked.

She nodded, blinked against the light, murmured something, and then went silent. Her hand hung limp against the sheet. I took it in mine. 'Oh Alice, please talk to me!'

'Where's Eamon? Why hasn't he come to see me?' she asked with a frown.

'I don't know where he is. The police haven't found him yet.'

'What will they do to him?' she asked fearfully.

'I don't know.' I shifted uneasily in my chair, watching her intently.

Her voice seemed to come from a great distance as she said, 'It wasn't his fault. He didn't do anything wrong, Ellie. He was sweet and kind to me; he made me feel wanted in a way I had never felt with Uncle Jack, Aunt Sally or Mary-Pat. He took me away from there because he knew that I couldn't stand it any longer.' She looked at me.

'Don't worry about all that now, just concentrate on getting better.'

'I wonder if he'll come to see me. Maybe he won't bother.'

With a bit of luck he'll be locked up, I thought, but said, 'He might not be able to visit you at the moment.'

She raised her eyebrows at me. 'I don't suppose so. Ellie, I didn't mean any harm.'

'Shh, don't tire yourself out.'

She closed her eyes, breathed deeply. I sat there in silence watching her while she shifted and moaned, wondering what could possibly have happened to her to put her in this state. Whatever it was had turned her world upside down, and ours too. There were so many things that I wanted to ask her, but now was not the time.

Aunt Sally arrived, stalking down the ward, a brittle smile on her face and a bag of grapes held aloft.

'You're looking much better,' she declared when Alice opened her eyes. 'Soon you'll be back to give us a hand. We've all the little jobs you used to do lying waiting, and Sister Catherine rang to say that everyone in the school is praying for you to get well.'

'I'm not going back there.' Alice turned away.

The nurse came to tell us that Doctor Martin would like to see us. As we entered his office he stood up, hesitant. 'Alice is suffering from a mental illness known as melancholia, or nervous debility,' he said.

'A grand way of saying she's mentally ill,' Aunt Sally said rudely.

He glared at her. 'Because of Alice's state of mind she became dependent on Eamon, and found herself in a very unhealthy situation—'

'I knew it was all her fault,' Aunt Sally interrupted.

Doctor Martin raised his hand. 'Also, this obsession resulted in a pregnancy.'

'What!' Aunt Sally gasped.

'Alice is not pregnant now, Mrs Casey. She's suffered a miscarriage, possibly through neglect, but luckily no physical damage has been done.'

Aunt Sally rolled her eyes. 'I don't believe any of this nonsense. I think you and the police are trying to build up a case against Eamon.'

Doctor Martin turned to her. 'I know it's a shock that she kept it a secret from you. But she panicked, as did your son Eamon when he discovered Alice's condition. So he agreed to take her away.' Doctor Martin looked at me.

'She's a manipulative little fool, using poor Eamon like that.' Aunt Sally was working herself up into a dramatic state, taking on the role of martyr.

'Don't you dare call her that,' I warned her.

Doctor Martin said, 'What your son did was wrong. What's more, he seems to have very little sense of responsibility.'

'How dare you!'

'I know you don't want to hear the truth about him. You just want to go on believing that he's your perfect son, but you'll hear it from the boy himself if the police find him, and it'll only be a matter of time until they do.'

Aunt Sally drew on her gloves. 'Thank you for your time, Doctor.'

'I'm staying with Alice for a while,' I said, wanting to flee from her, knowing the trouble that would arise as soon as we were alone.

'Suit yourself.' Aunt Sally, anxious and distrustful of what she'd just been told, left with a flustered expression on her face.

Back in the ward, Alice barely spoke to me. She just lay there staring into the distance as if she'd fallen into a trance. I longed to get out of there, go somewhere to be alone, so that I could think, and adjust gradually to this news. I wiped her face with a damp flannel, smoothed her hair, and plumped up her pillow. 'You have a good rest, Alice, I'm going for a walk,' I told her. 'I'll be back later.' She breathed a sigh of relief and turned into the pillow, glad to be left to sleep in peace.

I fled from the place, took the subway to Brighton Beach, desperate to get as far away from the hospital as I could.

Once there I walked along the boardwalk. The tide was going out. Sunlight slanted across the blue sea like a blade cutting through it.

I removed my shoes and stockings, and walked along the hard sand. A warm breeze blew over me as I hiked up my skirt and waded on in up to my thighs, feeling that same sense of abandon that Alice and I had felt when we'd paddled in the sea at home. I stared out at the expanse of blue waves and brilliant white foam, wondering if my little sister Alice still existed behind the frightened young woman in hospital. I stood watching the waves draw in the pebbles then fling them back with tremulous clamour, the long, withdrawing roar of the sea bringing a note of sadness that echoed my misery.

Back on the shore I sat on a rock and let the tears run down my cheeks, not bothering to wipe them as I thought of Alice, who should have been leading a normal life, going to school each day, getting on with her education. Now she would never return to school, not even to collect her things.

Gradually I reined in my feelings until I felt calm seeping back into me. Then I dried my eyes and walked back the way I'd come, determined that I wouldn't let Alice see my distress. I wouldn't let anyone know what I thought and felt. I would keep my feelings locked inside me.

Back at the house there were agitated voices, Aunt Sally's cries of dismay, Uncle Jack's loud, scolding voice, Mary-Pat whining. I sneaked upstairs and didn't come down until the following morning. Bridget insisted on cooking me breakfast while I brought her up to date on Alice's progress, then I scampered off to the hospital while Aunt Sally and Mary-Pat were still in bed.

Alice was much brighter. 'Ellie, I've something to tell you. It's important.'

'Can I ask you a question?'

'What?' Her eyes were guarded.

'How did you and Eamon get together?'

She smiled wanly. 'When he came to visit, I confided in him how much I hated it at Aunt Sally's. He told me that he too had a secret. He said that he'd dropped out of college because he hated it so much, and that he was working on one of the loading bays down at the docks to earn enough money to go to Canada. He made me swear not to tell a soul, and said that if Aunt Sally were to find out she'd go mad. He invited me to his place. I took the subway there. It was fun. He asked me to come and visit him again, told me not to tell anyone.'

'I'll bet he did. And then?'

She considered this question. 'I went back. He took me to the cinema and to the ice-cream parlour. I liked being with him. He had time for me. We fell in love, I guess.' An anxious look came over her face as she said, 'Ellie, I don't want you to think badly of him. He didn't make me do anything I didn't want to do. I knew exactly what I was doing.'

She looked as guilty as a child who'd misbehaved. I felt sorry for her.

'Ellie, there's something else,' she added.

'What is it?'

Her voice dropped and I had to lean forward to hear her. 'Swear you won't tell anyone.' I felt her fingers sliding into mine. Her eyes were on me. 'You have to swear it. Not a soul, especially not the police.'

'I swear that I won't tell a living soul,' I pledged.

'Eamon and I planned to get married. We were going to Canada; he's got a job there. Look, he gave me an engagement ring, said I couldn't wear it until we were in Canada.' She lifted a chain from around her neck that had been hidden beneath her hospital gown. It was a gold band with a tiny diamond hanging from it. 'Now I don't know what's going to happen,' she added, her deep concern making her miserable.

'You won't leave me until Eamon gets here, sure you won't, Ellie?' She spoke as if Eamon were detained somewhere on business.

'No, I'll stay with you,' I assured her, hoping that Eamon would soon be found, and made to pay for what he'd done to Alice.

Alice stared ahead, her eyes narrowed as if she was seeing her life empty of purpose without Eamon.

'Good.' She went silent then, withdrew into herself. It was as if she'd crossed some invisible line, into a world that excluded me.

I went to see her every day, dreading the visits because I couldn't bear to see her in such a state. Her only concern was for Eamon. She talked about him in a possessive, anxious way.

Concerned, I went to see Doctor Martin. 'Sometimes I look at her and it seems as if there's nothing there,' I told him. 'It's a frightening feeling, wondering if she'll ever be right again.'

'She will be right, but it will take time,' he assured me.

On the way to Aunt Sally's one day, I stopped at a market stall and bought a thin silver band for Alice to cheer her up. Knowing that I had to return to Boston before too long I bought a sketchpad and started on more designs for Mr Samuel's sportswear company, which I posted on to him. I had a little money to keep me going, but I couldn't go on as I was. My concern for Alice battled with my fear of financial ruin.

A few days later, Dora phoned to say that she was finding it very difficult to keep things going on her own – and I knew the time had come for me to return to Boston. Aunt Sally clearly wanted me to go. She said that she'd visit Alice every day. Not that I was consoled by that promise, because I knew that she'd upset Alice, but Bridget promised to keep an eye on Aunt Sally, and Alice too, and let me know how she was doing.

And so within a day or two I was back in Boston. Because of the length of time I'd been away stock was running out. With Dora's help I quickly got to work and made more hats. Though I spent as little money as possible, it wasn't coming in fast enough to keep us going. Sometimes when I went to pay a bill, my hands would tremble as I counted out the dollars, wondering how I would live for the rest of the week.

I phoned the hospital regularly to find out how Alice was, and was told that she was making good progress, and would soon be out. Foolishly I began to relax and think positively about the future . . . however uncertain it felt just then.

Eighteen

One evening the phone rang. It was Alice. She sounded very faint and far away.

'Alice, are you all right? I can hardly hear you,' I said.

'I'm in the Psychiatric Unit. I want you to come and take me out of here,' she said.

'I will, as soon as I can, I promise . . .'

'I want you to come for me now. I'm not staying here any longer.'

She was saying goodbye before I had a chance to have a proper talk with her.

Out of desperation I rang Aunt Sally. 'I heard from Alice, she sounded very disturbed.'

'She is disturbed. They've moved her to the Psychiatric Unit. You'd better come and see her,' she said in a resigned voice.

I left for Brooklyn immediately, telling Dora I would be back as soon as I could.

I approached the Psychiatric Unit of the hospital, scared, not knowing what state Alice would be in, or whether she would be allowed to see me. The waiting room smelled of antiseptic, the walls were dull, the upholstered chairs an orange-grey colour.

Eventually Alice came in to see me, walking carefully with a nurse beside her holding her arm. She looked thinner. Her hair was pulled back in a ponytail, making her cheekbones look sharper, and there was a bewildered look in her eyes.

'Hi, Alice,' I said.

She stood uncertainly, head to one side.

'Here's your sister,' the nurse said, smiling at me, giving her a gentle tug in my direction.

'I'm so glad to see you,' I said, giving her a kiss on the cheek. 'How are you?'

'Much better, aren't you, Alice? She's been looking forward to your visit, haven't you?' said the nurse, addressing her like a child.

'Yes.' She looked up at the nurse for approval.

I came forward, took her hand, settled her down into a chair beside mine.

'I'll leave you to have a little chat,' the nurse said, and left the room.

A woman in an overall brought in a tray. 'Coffee,' she said, placing it on a little table beside us.

'Thanks.' I poured out a cup for Alice. She fumbled with the handle of the cup, lifted it to her lips, then she put it down carefully.

'I hate it in here. They won't give me my clothes.'

'You're not well enough.'

'I haven't got anything of my own. And I'm tired all of time. It must be the pills they're giving me.' She gave me a lopsided grin.

'Oh, Alice, how did you get into this state?'

'I took some extra pills. I hid them each time I was given them and then took them all together.'

'Alice! Did you pass out?'

'Yes, I think so. The nurse found me. They pumped my stomach – made me vomit.' She began to cry. I felt tears well up in my eyes as I looked at her.

'I didn't want to go on without Eamon – Aunt Sally said he was never coming back to me.' Her voice was thick, hesitant. 'Oh, Ellie, you have to get me out of here. You don't know how awful it is,' she pleaded.

'I can't do that, Alice,' I said gently. 'You have to get well first, then you can leave.'

'It's like a prison. They ask all these questions, but I don't think they believe anything that I tell them.' She shook her head. 'There's nothing wrong with me. You know that. I heard Aunt Sally tell them to keep me in here. She hates me because of what happened. Now they'll never let me out. I'll be here for the rest of my life.'

I looked at her. Perhaps she was just shocked and traumatised – not mentally ill. Though there was no doubt that she was not herself, I prayed she'd get better, and was seething with fury at Aunt Sally's interference.

'So you won't get me out?' Alice asked.

'Well, I'll see what I can do.'

She sighed resignedly. 'You don't want me.'

'How can you say such a thing?'

'I'll get out anyway, and I'll go and find Eamon.' She had that old, defiant look in her eyes as she wobbled to her feet. I wanted to take her and shake her into reality. Remind her that she had a life of her own, and that she didn't need the likes of Eamon to mess it up. But there was no point. She wasn't rational.

I caught her arm. I walked her back down the corridor to the nurses' station. 'I'll come visit you tomorrow,' I said.

She began to cry. 'I'll take you back to Boston as soon as you're well enough, Alice, I promise.'

'She'll be all right once she's had a little rest,' the nurse said, taking her by the hand, leading her back to the dormitory.

As I left I heard the moaning and sudden cries of the patients trapped there, and the lonely swishing sound of the door closing behind me.

On the subway to Flatbush I thought of Alice locked up in that awful place, lost in her own confused world. What would happen if she were there for a long time? What if she didn't recover and required constant care for the rest of her life? Would I be able to look after her? Walking towards the house, I wished I had someone to talk to who would understand, and wondered how to tackle the fearsome Aunt Sally and what I would say when I got back.

As it turned out, it was Aunt Mabel who answered the door. Framed against it, tall and gracious in her sky-blue finery, she looked like an apparition.

'Aunt Mabel!' I stood gazing at her in amazement. I couldn't take it in. My greatest ally in the whole wide world, the one who'd always guided me with her love and devotion, was standing right there before me.

'Yes, it's me, darling,' she said softly.

'Oh, Aunt Mabel, I'm so glad to see you.' My throat tightened, my eyes swam with tears.

Her face shone with love as she stepped towards me. I fell into her arms, sobbing, unable to believe that she had turned up in Brooklyn, yet I probably should have expected it.

'There, there,' she soothed. 'I'm here now, everything will be all right.' She held me for a long time, neither of us saying a word. I realised how much I needed her.

Finally we broke apart. 'When did you get here?' I asked.

'This morning. I took one look at your letter and made up my mind there and then.'

'But you didn't write to tell me you were coming?'

'There wasn't time. Good Lord, Ellie! You knew I

wouldn't leave you to cope with Alice on your own,' she said, brushing away my tears with her fingertips. 'I came here to sort things out, and that's what I'll do. Come on in, there's so much I have to talk about. Let's sneak upstairs while Sally's resting, we'll have a bit of privacy there.'

Once in Alice's bedroom, Aunt Mabel closed the door and turned to me. 'Is Alice very ill?' she asked.

'Yes, and she's much worse since I saw her last.'

She sat down facing me, placed her hand on mine. 'Tell me everything. Start at the beginning,' she said gently.

I relayed the whole story to her, holding back none of the details; how Alice hadn't wanted to leave Eamon, how I'd grabbed the gun and escaped. As I talked, Aunt Mabel's face registered surprise, shock, anger, by turns as she listened. I finished by saying, 'I ran to the police.'

'That's how you got those bruises,' she said lifting my arm, looking at the patches of blue still there from Eamon's grasp.

'Yes. I thought Eamon was dead and that I had killed him, but the police haven't found his body.'

Aunt Mabel's hands flew to her face. 'Holy Mother of Divine Jesus!' she exclaimed.

'Oh Aunt Mabel, I had to get Alice away from Eamon, I was afraid he would destroy her,' I sobbed. 'But he's disappeared . . . or he's dead. When the police find his body I'll be thrown into jail for the rest of my life.' My secret was out. For the first time in weeks I gave in to my despair. I sank down on my knees before her. 'I've ruined everything; I am so sorry, Aunt Mabel.'

'You poor thing, and poor little Alice,' she said, holding me tight. 'You haven't killed Eamon, he's escaped. Take it from me, he was always a sly one but I never thought he was evil. Alice was easy prey for him. She always had a wild streak, running off, climbing trees, hiding up in one for as long as she could get away with it.'

'So she wouldn't have to help with the housework,' I added with a weak smile.

'Lord knows we used to have to chastise her often, but she's a good girl really. She certainly doesn't deserve this.'

I closed my eyes, pictured Alice high up in a tree, me calling up to her to come down at once, that it was growing dark. I thought of her adventurous spirit and wondered if Eamon had broken it. When I opened them Aunt Mabel was gazing out of the window, her eyes focused on the sky. I had no idea what she was thinking. 'Ellie, how are Jack and Sally with Alice now?' she asked.

'Uncle Jack is too mad to talk to her; Aunt Sally yells at her all the time, and at everyone else too. Alice told me that Aunt Sally asked the doctor in charge to keep her in the hospital. I hate her, and I hate Uncle Jack because he won't stand up to her. And Mary-Pat treated

Alice badly too.' The words came out strangled and high-pitched.

'What a nerve that woman has!' Aunt Mabel slid up beside me and took me in her arms.

The tears gathered as I said, 'It all seems so strange now, like a dream.'

'A nightmare.' I could tell from her tightened jaw that she was mad as hell.

The atmosphere grew quiet.

'Aunt Mabel, I'm so frightened for Alice. What's going to happen to her?' A barrier seemed to break and suddenly the floodgates opened, the tears gushed down.

Her arms enclosed me. She pressed me to her bosom. 'Oh you poor child, cry as much as you like, you've been through the mill, I know how much it hurts.' Fresh tears erupted as she held me, all my pent-up fears coming to the surface. I cried like the rain, soaking her suit with my tears. She held me tight and rocked me back and forth, murmuring soothing words, until my sobs slowed down to shuddering breaths. Finally, I pulled back. Aunt Mabel tilted my chin. 'This is all a terrible mess but we're going to sort it out, everything's going to be all right. I'm here now, you can relax.'

Her hands were warm as she held mine; her face was full of kindness. She stroked my hair like she used to do when I was a child. 'Don't worry about Alice. She'll not be left to rot in that hospital. I'll go and see her doctor tomorrow. Talk to her psychiatrist, get a proper diagnosis.' Her capable voice promised that she would take care of everything as she dried my eyes with her lace handkerchief.

'Are you here for long?'

'As long as it takes for Alice to get well enough to travel. I'm taking her back to Ireland with me,' she said matter-of-factly.

'Oh!' The problem was solved for me. Alice was going back to Ireland. I should have been delighted but, instead, a light feeling went through me like a long, sad sigh.

'What about your shop? Who's looking after it?'

'Peggy's cousin, Mary Murphy, is running it until I get back. She trained in a haberdashery back in Lisdoonvarna.'

'But you might be here for some time.'

'I have whatever time it'll take to get Alice better, though God knows how I'll put up with Sally while I'm here. She gives me the creeps.'

'Alice and I used to hide up here when she hit the roof. Sometimes we felt so small in this big house, it was as if it closed in on us, dragged us down.'

It was peaceful alone with Mabel, and pleasant to sit there in the late afternoon, at the top of the house with her, the old glow of childhood conspiracy back with the twinkle in her eye, the gaiety not far beneath the surface.

★　★　★

Downstairs, it seemed so strange to have Aunt Mabel under the same roof as Aunt Sally, who hovered in the background like a malevolent witch.

Uncle Jack arrived, tramping in, shocked at the sight of Aunt Mabel, his eyes wary as he greeted her.

'Have you been here long, Mabel?' he asked finally.

'Arrived this morning.'

'Why didn't you let us know you were coming?' he said cautiously.

'It was a snap decision, there wasn't time.'

'Ellie sent for her,' Aunt Sally chided me.

'No she didn't. I made up my mind to come when I heard what had happened to Alice. It was such a shock to us all at home,' she said knotting her fingers together, a worried expression on her face. 'I knew you'd find it hard to cope, Sally, what with your bad nerves and everything.'

I felt uncomfortable. It was obvious that neither one of them cared for the other.

Aunt Sally backed away, saying that she needed a cigarette. Uncle Jack went to have a bath and change for dinner, and Mabel and I went down to the kitchen to chat to Bridget.

Dinner was a disaster. I knew there was going to be trouble. I could feel it brewing as we sat around the table uneasily, eating in silence, the web of unpleasantness among us all tangible. Uncle Jack asked Aunt

Mabel about her journey, while Aunt Sally offered her more soup. Aunt Mabel, her cheeks flushed, said finally, 'I suppose we're all going to sit here and pretend that nothing's wrong.' Her eyes moved from Aunt Sally to Uncle Jack. They looked up at her, their mouths open. 'We all know something terrible has happened in this family. Are we not going to discuss it?' she told them.

Aunt Sally fiddled with her knife and fork while Uncle Jack cast a bitter glance at Mabel. 'Sure we are, but not right now, we're having dinner,' he said.

'Yes, and in comfort, while Alice is in hospital having a nervous breakdown – according to you, Sally.'

'That's what they suppose. But who knows what that means exactly.' Uncle Jack raised an eyebrow at her. 'I reckon she's just being stubborn, wanting to get her own way as usual.'

'I reckon she's lost her sanity,' said Aunt Sally.

Aunt Mabel looked at her with resentment. 'For God's sake, Sally, don't overdramatise!' she exploded with surprising violence.

Aunt Sally drew a long breath, 'I was just saying—'

Aunt Mabel turned challengingly to her. 'Haven't you said enough already? Done enough damage, asking the doctors to keep her hospitalised?'

'If she really is mentally ill, then she needs to be institutionalised,' Uncle Jack said.

'If she does, it's all your fault, and you'll take the rap,' Aunt Mabel said to him.

'For God's sake don't blame Jack,' Aunt Sally said.

Aunt Mabel sat up straight. 'You both are responsible for what's happened to Alice.'

'We're suffering too, our family's falling apart all because of that stupid child's antics,' retorted Aunt Sally. 'We don't even know where Eamon is!' Her voice rose. She turned to Uncle Jack. 'And what have you done about finding him? The cops don't seem to be making much progress.'

'What do you expect me to do about it right now while I'm having dinner?' asked Uncle Jack. 'Tomorrow I'll go see Mayor Walker. I guarantee you he'll do everything he can to help.'

'I need to see Eamon, I need to know that he's all right.' She clutched her handkerchief to her bosom in a theatrical way. 'I never imagined that anything like this could happen.' She turned to Aunt Mabel. 'This is all your doing, not Jack's,' she said, pointing a menacing finger at her.

'How's that?' Aunt Mabel faced her.

'It was you who persuaded Jack to take in your nieces. You told him that they were good, hard-working girls, and you promised that they would be no trouble at all.'

'That's exactly what they are, good girls. But then the pair of you got your hands on them . . .'

'We did our best for them, we gave them a home, and they thanked us by running off,' Aunt Sally protested.

'You did not do your best,' Aunt Mabel countered.

'You made life hell for them. Ellie and Alice were brave girls, doing *their* best, and you crushed their spirit, and made them unhappy. Didn't it make you feel guilty making them work like that when they needed a bit of nurturing, being so far away from home?' she asked.

Uncle Jack shot her a guilty look. 'I couldn't have afforded to keep them for nothing,' he said lamely.

'Rubbish, that's an excuse. You're making plenty of money.'

Aunt Sally's eyes filled with tears. 'They never appreciated anything I did for them. Ellie thanked us by running off, and Alice just wasted her time at school, and then disappeared.'

Aunt Mabel knitted her brows together. 'I'd have run off too if I'd been treated the way you treated them. You're an empty-hearted woman, Sally, who can't conceive of love. You bossed them around, made them do everything. They were too scared of you to disobey. And as for you, Jack, I don't believe you gave a damn about either of your nieces since they set foot on American soil. You just used them for your own benefit. Ellie did the work willingly because it was what she felt she should to secure an education. And you deprived her of that.'

I could hear the intake of Uncle Jack's breath. Aunt Sally gave a strangled sob, picked up her glass of wine and left the room. A door banged upstairs.

Uncle Jack picked up his knife and fork and

continued eating as if nothing had happened, but it was obvious that he was fuming, and I was delighted. Aunt Mabel was the first person to stand up to him in the house since I'd arrived, and it was about time. This fact wasn't lost on Mary-Pat either. She dropped her sullen look and sat up straight, and respectful.

Finally, Uncle Jack pushed his chair back and stood up from the table and sloped off, mumbling something about checking to see if Aunt Sally was all right. Mary-Pat followed meekly behind him.

Aunt Mabel sat back and breathed a sigh of relief. 'Well, do you think that I was cruel enough to them?' she asked mischievously, sounding very pleased with herself.

'I think you were wonderfully cruel,' I said gleefully as I began to stack the plates. I took them down to the kitchen. Bridget was waiting for me.

'I heard the rumpus up above,' she said quietly as she began to wash the plates.

'Yes, Aunt Mabel let them know what she thought of them.'

'Well, they've got away with far too much already. What's going to happen next, I wonder?'

'I don't know. I just hope Alice gets better soon so that we can get out of here.'

Aunt Mabel and I went up to bed as soon as the dishes were done. I could hear Aunt Mabel's comforting breathing as I said my prayers, asking God to make Alice better soon. If he did it would be a sign, proof that he cared for us, as we had always believed.

Nineteen

The following morning, Aunt Mabel and I went to see Alice. She was lying in her bed, her eyes tight shut, and her arms limply by her sides.

'Hello, Alice,' Aunt Mabel said softly.

Alice opened her eyes. When she saw Aunt Mabel standing there, she blinked as if trying to wake up.

'It's me, Alice.'

Alice pulled herself up. 'Is it really you?' she asked groggily.

Aunt Mabel's face softened and her eyes filled with tears. 'Oh, you poor, darling child!' She reached forward and took her in her arms, and held her while Alice sobbed. 'I'm here now, and you're going to be all right,' she assured her.

'Yes, but I'm so scared, Aunt Mabel.'

'What are you scared of?'

'Everything – doors opening suddenly, and noise. I think I'm losing my mind.'

'No you're not. You've had a terrible, traumatic time. It will ease.'

'I'm so worried about Eamon, I don't know what's happened to him.' Alice's voice was bleak and desolate, her eyes blurred.

'We don't know, either, he seems to have vanished but I'm sure the police will find him.'

'Oh! I just hope he's all right.' Alice bit her lip.

Aunt Mabel reached out and took her hand, held it tight. 'I'm sure he is. Meantime, you must be brave,' she said reassuringly. 'When you're stronger we'll talk about it all. I have so much to tell you. Your mam sends her love, and Lucy, and so do Ed and Maura. Oh, you should see little Brendan. He's racing around the place, a real livewire. And Matthew, your little brother, is gorgeous. Wait till you see him.'

Alice's eyes brightened. 'Oh, I'd give anything to see him.'

'You will see him as soon as you're better because I'm taking you back to Ireland with me.'

Alice's face clouded over. 'But I can't go, Aunt Mabel. I want to be here when Eamon gets back. He'll be looking for me.'

'It'll only be for a holiday, and not until you're feeling up to it. Eamon will be back by then I'm sure,' said Aunt Mabel skilfully back-pedalling.

'Really! Oh, that'll be great.' Alice was smiling at last. It was as if she'd forgotten everything she'd gone through.

The Ward Sister came bustling into the ward. 'Alice

is so much better today, so much stronger.'

Alice did seem brighter, but tiredness came over her after a while, confusing her speech, and her thoughts. She lay back on her pillows, exhausted. I stayed with her while Aunt Mabel went off with the nurse to see Doctor Martin.

On the way back to Uncle Jack's, Aunt Mabel pulled out her handkerchief and dabbed her eyes. 'I could murder that Eamon for what he's done to her, I really could, Ellie,' she said.

'So could I. But nobody could have foreseen that this would happen,' I said gently.

'Doctor Martin thinks Alice's unhealthy obsession with him will only be cured when he returns and rejects her. Then she will realise that she must forget all about him.'

'Let's hope they find him soon then, and that Alice recovers and regains her confidence.'

'She will once she gets back to Ireland and with the family again, she'll be fine,' she said in her practical way.

'It might take time.'

She turned to me suddenly. 'I'll wait. Meantime, I'll go back to Boston with you, come to see your store.'

'Oh, Aunt Mabel, that would be lovely, but I'm not sure there will be a store for much longer. It's been badly neglected.'

'We'll soon get it going again,' she said with a confident smile.

The morning we left for Boston was bright with sunshine. In a black suit and crisp white blouse Aunt Mabel briskly packed her suitcase while Uncle Jack stood, white and sharp-faced, announcing that he would personally drag her through the entire United States judiciary system if she attempted to slur his name and character to anyone. Aunt Mabel ignored him.

We stopped by at the hospital first. Aunt Mabel promised Alice that she'd be back at the weekend to see her. Then we took the train to Boston, Aunt Mabel smiling happily all the way.

When we arrived she jumped out on to the platform full of excitement, the old Mabel, as prankish and carefree as a girl. 'I can't help it, Ellie. I was never anywhere except New York last time I was in America.'

I herded her out of the station and into a cab that took us to the store. It delighted her. 'What a lovely place you have,' she said, looking around at the drapes and cushions, impatient to see everything.

Dora was in the workroom. 'This is my Aunt Mabel.' I introduced her proudly.

'I'm pleased to make your acquaintance, I'm sure, I've heard so much about you,' Dora said, standing up to shake Aunt Mabel's hand.

'And I've heard all about you too, and how good you've been to Ellie in these difficult times.'

'I only did what anyone would do, but as you see I'm

running out of hats, and the customers are complaining,' said Dora.

'We'll have to do something about that,' said Aunt Mabel, going to stand at the counter, restlessly looking around at the half-empty shelves.

'And, by the way, Shirlee gave birth to a baby girl while you were away,' Dora announced, smiling.

'Oh, how wonderful!' I was overcome with joy for Shirlee and Mr Samuel, and sad I hadn't been able to go and visit her.

'Cheer up, Ellie, things will be fine,' Dora said kindly, seeing the expression on my face.

The next day we went to the supplier's, where Aunt Mabel picked out the most expensive material and trims, and we set to work.

First, Aunt Mabel rearranged the store. She draped lengths of silk and damask into folds, matching the colours with reels of thread – pink, indigo and chestnut – so that a customer could see for herself what our new autumn range comprised. Then she went down to the antique store and bought a gramophone and a pile of records, and set up camp in the workroom making hats, her needle flicking neatly in and out as she stitched to the rhythm of 'Potato Head Blues' or a jazz tune. We made purple felt hats with fake fruit, crimson smokestacks with black netting, and some with ostrich feathers.

Dora spent most of the time helping customers

choose their hat from my illustrations, while we worked fast to have them ready on time.

Aunt Mabel, too, made her acquaintance with each client, delving into their history in the most unobtrusive way, offering special deals for weddings, christenings, funerals. It was like old times. Seeing the steadily increasing figures entered in the columns of the account book, I felt a flare of excitement and saw the promise of the life I had planned.

Mr Samuel phoned and I congratulated him on the birth of his daughter. 'Oh, she's a beauty!' He sounded delighted. 'I'll be in to collect more designs as soon as Shirlee lets me out of the house,' he joked.

Violet came to meet Aunt Mabel. After the introductions, I drew her aside to enquire about Zak.

'He's gone – given in his notice at the bank and taken a sabbatical for a few months.'

'But where to?'

'Travelling. Oh, I miss him but at least he's doing what he always wanted to do. Of course his parents think it was a terrible decision, but fulfilment is the most important thing, don't you think?'

'Yes, but why did he suddenly take off when things were going so well for him?'

'There was the pressure his mother put on him to marry Gloria. He couldn't take it any more.' There was sadness in her voice as she spoke.

'Maybe he'd have been better off with Gloria.'

'No, Ellie, he has never been in love with Gloria. You know nothing ever happened between them.' She was watching me carefully.

'How do you know?'

'Because he told me so.'

'Why didn't he tell me?'

Violet placed a hand on my shoulder. 'Ellie, he tried to and you wouldn't listen.'

'Because she was always around, popping up everywhere.'

'Yes I know, and he felt trapped by her. He would have done anything to get away from her sometimes. Not that he ever said that. He wouldn't – he was too loyal to his family.'

It was the first time I had heard her sound so certain about Zak. I didn't know what to say, didn't know where to begin.

For a moment it was as if a great weight had been lifted from me. My head felt light with relief at what Violet had just said. But what was I doing filling my head with romantic notions about Zak when it was too late? He was gone. However much I longed for him I couldn't allow myself to think about him in that way again. It wasn't possible.

I began to cry, and couldn't stop. I cried for what I'd lost in realising too late how unimportant Gloria was to him. But most of all I cried for myself, for not trusting him, and now he'd gone.

Violet put her arms around me. 'Gosh, Ellie, you're finally going to admit to me that you love him.'

I didn't say anything. There was nothing to say.

'He'll come back,' she consoled me.

I wasn't so sure, and even if he did there was no guarantee that it would be me he would come back to. I couldn't bring myself to tell Aunt Mabel about him so I kept my heartache to myself.

At the end of the week Aunt Mabel returned to New York to visit Alice, and was back on the Sunday evening with the news that Alice was making good progress and that her mind was now on her trip home. She rarely spoke of Eamon and seemed less anxious about everything. 'How's business?' she asked, after all that.

'Every hat in the place has been sold!' I told her.

'Don't tell me that, Ellie, you're making it up,' she protested.

'No, honestly, see for yourself.'

'I'll bet that you've given half of them away just to impress me,' she laughed.

'It's the truth, Aunt Mabel. The ladies loved the new styles. We've no stock left.'

'We'll have to make more.'

Mr Samuel came to collect more sportswear designs. He was smiling from ear to ear as he told me about the orders that were pouring in for his swimsuits. 'We're drowning in them.' He laughed at his own pun.

I introduced him to Aunt Mabel, who said, 'Oh how marvellous to meet you, simply marvellous,' making far too much of him.

A delighted Mr Samuel turned to me and said, 'By the way, Ellie, Shirlee wants you to be godmother to baby Crystal.'

I flushed. 'I'd be honoured, of course. But I'm not Jewish, I'm a Catholic, Mr Samuel.'

'So's Shirlee, if a bit lapsed. It's going to be a Catholic christening. It's what Shirlee wants. Between you and me I think that she wants to make amends. The two of you were so close. She misses you. I'll be the outsider at this one,' he replied good-humouredly.

'Well, I accept – how wonderful!'

'Great.' He smiled. 'I've sent an invitation to Zak,' he added casually.

'You did?'

'Well, it's his money I'm spending, might as well keep him sweet.'

'He's away at present, he mightn't be able to make it.'

'Oh well, I'll see him when he gets back.'

The fact that I couldn't share this news with Zak took some of the pleasure out of it. I never thought it was possible to miss someone so much. I couldn't believe that he wasn't going to phone me up to invite me to a jazz concert, or walk through the door with a bunch of flowers and make some snide remark about me working too hard. I wanted to see him so badly I couldn't sleep at night. When the persistent ache of longing for him wouldn't go I wrote him a letter, but tore it up.

The christening was held at Saint Stephen's Roman Catholic Church. I wore my white broderie anglaise frock, pinned a bunch of violets on the shoulder, and made a violet-coloured bandeau with a wide feather to match it. Aunt Mabel looked divine in a turquoise silk creation, with a gold fringe wrap, and a hat with ostrich feathers that zoomed to the sky. She sailed up the aisle with the ostrich feathers fluttering like a bird in flight, me nervously behind her.

The high altar was draped in a long, white lace cloth, and decked with lillies and racks of tall white candles. Shirlee's family crowded the front pews; Shirlee's mother, in a fuchsia-pink suit and tiny hat, looked proud, her father with brushed back hair, and a fierce look in his eyes as if he were ready to fight anyone who challenged him. Her brothers and sisters were all scrubbed up and shining.

Mr Samuel's puzzled-looking father sat to one side, acting as if the Catholic church was the most mysterious place he'd ever been in.

Shirlee, in a magnificent black-and-white dress, and wearing a hat covered in black and white silk flowers, made a dramatic entrance, proudly carrying her baby. Mr Samuel and David, delightful in a navy-and-white sailor suit, followed. Arnie Walker, a tall, craggy-faced man who introduced himself with a beaming smile as the second godfather took my arm and walked me up to the baptism font to the swell of the organ, where we faced the priest in white robes.

'Thank you for this,' Shirlee whispered, her eyes sparkling as she handed me baby Crystal, a beautiful, tiny thing in a long silk robe, sleeping peacefully, her thumb in her mouth, blissfully unaware of the fuss that was going on in her honour.

Mr Samuel stood beaming by the font, Shirlee beside him, her face composed in a saintly expression as the priest said the sacred words, 'I baptise you, Crystal Ruth,' and poured water over her forehead. I felt a shiver go through her body, and imagined that the Holy Spirit was flitting into her soul. Then the choir sang '*Panis Angelicas*', waking her up and making her cry.

Once outside I handed Crystal back to Shirlee, who said, 'Thanks, Ellie. I'm so grateful you agreed to be godmother, and so sorry we fell out.'

'So am I,' I said, giving her a big hug.

Everyone wanted a peek at the baby, some even reaching out to touch her as Shirlee got in the car with Mr Samuel and drove off.

Back at the house the patio soon filled with people; ladies sipping drinks, and the men smoking cigars. Aunt Mabel was in her element, drifting around, chatting to the guests as if she'd known them all of her life. The men kept glancing at her, impatient for her company.

Two maids in uniform appeared and passed around trays of dainty sandwiches, cocktail sausages, shrimp and cress. Shirlee caught sight of me and came over. 'Ellie, it's so lovely to have you here,' she said, giving my hand a squeeze, none of the tension of my last visit apparent. Before I had a chance to have a proper chat with her Arnie was over, Mr Samuel on his heels.

'Gawd, you're nothing like what I expected – you're so young. Nice to see such young people getting involved in the business,' he beamed.

'And she's very talented too,' Mr Samuel told him proudly.

'Sammy showed me your designs. I'm very impressed.'

Bowled over by his compliment, all I could say was a meek 'Thank you'.

'Did I mention that Arnie's head buyer in Macy's? He's interested in placing a very large order.' Mr Samuel winked at me.

'That's wonderful,' I said, delighted.

'Thing is, I'll want an exclusive on them, Sammy, and seeing as you're charging enough for them I think I'm entitled to that.'

I looked questioningly at Mr Samuel. 'Oh! I don't know about that. I've had great interest from several of the other big stores.'

'Well, let's not worry about details like that right now, we can iron them out later.'

Under an oak tree David was on a swing, shrieking with delight, his blond hair flying as he was being pushed by a little girl.

Shirlee came on the scene. 'I'm going to feed Crystal – coming?'

As soon as she shut the door of the nursery, she said, 'I'm sorry I was so touchy about the trip to Paris. I guess I was feelin' bad the way Sammy sprung it on me an' all.'

'I understand, I didn't like to think of you being left behind either. I'm sorry too,' I said.

'I was overreacting, as usual. Things were a little difficult between us then. Hell, I don't want to go through it again. If I ever start getting broody remind me I said that.' She was almost in tears.

'Sure will,' I laughed.

Our eyes met. Shirlee smiled. 'I missed you, honey,' she said as she picked up Crystal, and snuggled her head against her breast.

'I missed you too.'

'Sammy wanted her first name to be Ruth after his mom, but I insisted on naming her after Ma.'

'She's really cute, Shirlee,' I said, totally smitten with the beautiful child.

'She's good, too. Not that she lets me get much sleep at night, but Sammy helps out more these days.'

'Things better between the two of you now?'

Shirlee gave a small laugh. 'Sure, we're in a better place right now, and I've learned to make the most of things. I've got everything I want, two beautiful children, a beautiful home, and he's promised to take me to Paris for the spring fashion shows over there.' She paused, a look of uncertainty on her face, and then changed the subject. 'How d'ya like the way I had the nursery decorated?' she asked, running a hand over the side of the most elaborate white cot I'd ever seen.

We stayed chatting cosily for a while when Shirlee said, 'By the way, where's your Zak?'

'Oh, he's not my Zak,' I corrected her.

'Have you two fallen out?'

'No, not at all, he's gone off travelling,' I told her.

'Are you OK with that?'

'Oh, fine.'

I could see that Shirlee didn't believe me, but she left it alone. Eventually Jewel came in to take Crystal, so we went back downstairs to join the party.

Aunt Mabel was sitting at a table, chatting with Arnie, both of them looking enchanted with one another. I sensed something different in Aunt Mabel, something indefinable in her demeanour, and a new brightness that hadn't been there before.

As soon as we appeared, Mr Samuel called for silence.

'We're all here this afternoon to celebrate the birth of our beautiful daughter, Crystal. She's an angel, and so is her mother.' He walked over to stand beside Shirlee. 'To my family,' he said, raising his glass. There was a burst of applause as everyone raised their glasses. An enormous cake frosted in white and pink was brought in. Mr Samuel picked up a knife and he and Shirlee held hands as they cut it. The guests erupted.

I looked around the room, buzzing with people spilling out on to the corridor, wishing that Zak were among them. If only I could see him again then the ache inside me would vanish.

Over the next few days Aunt Mabel was full of chat about the wonderful party and the even-more-wonderful Arnie, so when he phoned her, inviting her out to dinner, it came as no surprise to Dora and me. By the time she was leaving for New York to visit Alice, Arnie was insisting on driving her there in his motorcar.

Twenty

On the Saturday evening I was walking back to the store, thinking about Alice. I was wondering how she was when I heard someone call out 'Ellie?'

I turned and saw Johnny Sheerin standing there, a suitcase in his hand. Thinking I was dreaming, I went up to take a closer look.

'Johnny?' With a shock of pleasure I took a couple of steps nearer. 'Is it really you?'

'It's me.' His black hair sprang back from his thin face, and there was a dark blue shadow on his lower cheeks and jaw. But the smile that lit up his whole face filled me with joy at seeing him again.

'What are you doing here?'

'What do you think? I've come to visit you. I've just arrived.'

'Come on in.' As he walked in ahead of me I took in his strong back, his long legs, even the familiar shoes and socks he wore, with a sense of disbelief.

'Would you like coffee, a drink?' The words stumbled out.

'A cup of coffee would be great,' he said, standing to one side of the kitchen, looking around.

'Come and sit down.'

My hands were shaking as I made the coffee, but in spite of the emotion of him being here I couldn't help wondering why he'd come.

'Here we are,' I said, setting down the percolator, fetching the milk and sugar and mugs.

He leaned back, crossing his legs in an easy, relaxed way as I poured the coffee.

'I'm sorry I didn't let you know I was coming. I made my mind up so quickly that I didn't have time to write to you.'

'You've nothing to be sorry about. I'm really glad to see you.'

There was silence as we sipped our coffee, then Johnny said, 'I heard from Mabel that you'd been through a rough time with Alice, and that that was why she was coming over. I was very anxious about you.'

'Aunt Mabel has been wonderful. I couldn't have managed without her. And Alice is recovering, thank God. That's not why you've come, is it?'

'No, my brother, Liam, has got work for me on a ranch in Texas. I thought I'd try my luck at making that pot of gold we all hear about. And I had to get away from things back home.'

'What has been happening? You can't have been mixed up in the civil war still?'

His face was masked in shadow. I looked at him, trying to gauge the situation. 'Why did you really come here, Johnny?' I asked him out straight.

The silence grew louder. Finally, he said, hesitatingly, 'The Troubles are still going on, and I'm a wanted man.'

'What!'

'Ellie, the mistake people make is in thinking that the civil war is over. It isn't by any means. The Troubles have spilled over into the new Free State Army now, and there aren't really any changes. They're looking for the men who carried guns before the treaty was signed in London, and all the lads of my age are under surveillance.'

'The Irregulars, you mean.'

'Yes, that treaty in London should never have been signed.'

'Maybe so, but surely war is the worst thing.'

He nodded. 'Yes, but that's the point – it's still going on. My Uncle Danny was arrested for being involved in the burning out of one of the big houses owned by a member of the Free State Senate. It's only a matter of time before they'll link me to him.'

'Oh no! And what about Ed? Is he in danger?'

'Yes, Ed too is being watched because of his involvement. All of the youngsters in our village were involved, and who could blame them?' His fighting words filled me with dread thinking of Ed still at risk.

'What about his wife Maura, and baby Brendan, and Mam and Lucy living on the farm with them? Will they be at risk too?'

'Ed'll be all right. He's going up for town councillor to prove that he's on the side of the Free State, and good for him.'

'I hate to talk of war, Johnny. It frightens me.'

'Ellie, it was our chance to do what we could for our country at the time, and we did it. I don't expect you to understand,' he continued without expression. 'It wasn't your fault that you didn't know what was happening. Your dad made sure you were kept out of it. You lived in a little world of your own at the time.'

'That's true. I used to feel guilty about it when I saw what Ed was going through.'

'You've nothing to feel guilty about. You worked hard, and you were very responsible towards your family. God knows, they suffered enough, it was a terrible hard time for your mam when your dad drowned.'

'It doesn't help to go over and over things.' I cast my eyes downwards, and bit my lip to stop the unwanted tears as I recalled the day Dad's body was found. It was as vivid in my mind as if it had happened yesterday.

Johnny put his hand on mine in an effort to offer sympathy. I trembled as I felt its warmth spread up my arm. 'I'm sorry I upset you bringing it all back like that, but it's all in the past for me now, Ellie, I've done with it.' His palm closed over my knuckles, his strong hand held on to mine as he bowed his head. All I could see of his face was his sharp cheekbones, the ridge of his nose, and the strong pulse that beat in his neck. When he lifted his eyes to look at me it was like he was making a pledge with me.

'I'm glad to hear it.' I folded my fingers into his and he smiled.

'Now tell me all your news,' he said.

For the next hour I talked to Johnny more intimately about my life and myself than I'd ever talked to anyone. I told him all about Alice running away, and my search for her, my run-in with Eamon, and Alice's breakdown. He listened, his eyes on me all the time that I spoke, his face full of attention, as if there was nothing else more interesting to him in the world.

When I finished I glanced up at him. His face was stern as he said, 'I know what I'd like to do to that cousin of yours if I ever got my hands on him.'

'I hope you never meet him. I'd prefer to let the law take care of him.'

Johnny smiled. 'Fair enough.'

'What about dinner? You must be starving.'

'Let me take you out for a meal, save you having to cook.'

Johnny showered and returned to the kitchen fully dressed, his wet hair a tangle of curls, his shoulder blades sharp as wings beneath his snow-white shirt.

* ★ ★

Outside, the street was buzzing with people. The evening air was heavy with the smell of garlic and other herbs, the restaurants busy. Finally we found an Italian restaurant with a vacant table.

'Will this do?' I asked him.

'I've always fancied trying something different,' he said, excited. I looked at him, examining the menu. We settled for a ravioli dish.

When the waiter had taken the order and left, Johnny said, 'Ellie, I'm sorry, really sorry.'

'What about?'

'For upsetting you, talking about the Troubles. You've been through enough recently without bringing all that back into your life,' he said.

'I'm not upset now, I'm so happy that you're here.'

'Me too.' He took my hand firmly in his, squeezed it, his eyes devouring me as if he could never get enough of looking at me.

Outside, the street lamp cast shadows beneath us as we walked along. He tilted his head towards mine. The touch of his shoulder against my cheek burned into me.

Back home, the hallway echoed in the silence. In the kitchen, Johnny moved around restlessly.

'Listen, you can sleep on the sofa,' I told him.

'I don't have to stay with you, Ellie, I'll get a room in a downtown hotel for a couple of days.'

'No, you stay. Tomorrow you can look for a room if you want to.'

He looked at me anxiously. 'Are you sure it won't set the neighbours talking if I stay here?' The light fell on his face, which looked older suddenly, and exhausted.

'What neighbours? It's all business premises around here. We're the only ones living above the shop. Anyway Dora'll be back tomorrow, so we'll be respectable.'

He laughed. I made tea from the supplies he'd brought me from Mam, and we sat talking, laughing when our conversation turned towards our childhood pranks, when I noticed that Johnny's eyes were closing.

'I think it's time we said goodnight,' I said, smiling at him.

'Yes, I'm sorry but I'm all in.'

At the door of the workroom I handed him a pillow and sheet and told him to make himself comfortable. He stood there, his arms hanging limply by his sides. 'Thanks, Ellie,' he said.

I hesitated for a fraction of a second, wanting to tell him how truly glad I was to see him, but shyness overtook me.

'You're welcome. Goodnight, Johnny.'

He didn't move, just stood watching me go upstairs.

Hours passed before I slept because I was so conscious of Johnny being downstairs. All the memories his presence brought raced round in my head, and I felt sad thinking of what he'd been through, fighting for his country – things he hadn't talked about. I wondered about the future, and what his plans were, and if his arrival would change things.

I must have fallen into a deep sleep because when I awoke the next morning I was convinced that I had been dreaming that Johnny was here. Gradually, it dawned on me that it wasn't a dream and that he was downstairs sleeping on my couch.

I got up and went down into the workroom, and tiptoed to the sofa. He was fast asleep – a tangle of arms and legs wrapped up in the sheet. A strip of sunlight lay on his face, which in repose looked perfect, and beautiful under the dark web of hair upon the pillow; his collarbone jutted out, and his flesh was so fine that I could see a map of veins. His eyes flickered, stirring something protective in me. I thought of the passion in his kisses when we were parting after my holiday back home, how he'd held my gaze in his as he'd begged me to stay on. It all seemed like a lifetime ago.

I closed the door gently behind me to go into the kitchen to prepare breakfast.

'Ellie!' he called.

I opened it again. He was propped on one elbow, peering at me. 'Top of the mornin' to you,' he smiled.

'Good morning, Johnny. Did you sleep well?'

'Like a log, best sleep I've had since I left Ireland.'

'Good. I'll start breakfast?'

He rubbed his eyes, blinked. 'Great!' he said.

'Are you going to have a look around Boston?' I asked him half an hour later as I put the plate of bacon and eggs down in front of him.

Johnny reached for my hand. 'Ellie, why don't you come with me, show me the sights?'

'I'm busy trying to catch up on the orders, Johnny.'

'Sorry, I shouldn't have asked.'

'That's OK. Tell you what, why don't I invite my friend Violet round this evening for dinner? You'd like her.'

I phoned Violet to invite her round; explaining to her the big surprise it was to see Johnny on the doorstep.

'Wow! I'll bet!' she said, madly excited at the prospect of meeting him.

She took to him instantly, and we had a wonderful evening with Dora, and Violet showing Johnny how to jitterbug.

The next few days were great fun. Johnny spent the days sightseeing, but he and I spent the evenings together. We went to the local restaurants, lingering over our meal, returning to the store, where we talked the night away.

Each morning I would rise and tiptoe downstairs and peep into the workroom to watch him sleeping, hardly believing that he was there.

One morning, he watched me in silence as I made a

pot of coffee. He took the mug gratefully, blew on his drink before he took a sip.

'So, is there someone in your life, Ellie?' he asked.

I hesitated. 'Well, there is somebody . . . But I'm not sure . . .'

'I hope he's . . . suitable.' He said it protectively. 'Is he?'

'He's handsome and charming.'

'I'm not concerned about what he looks like,' he said huskily. He looked at me with a mock-fierce expression. 'If he doesn't take care of you he might find me handy with my fists.'

'Oh, Johnny!' I laughed, tossing a cushion at him. 'Come on, let's pack up your bedding.' We smiled at each other, friends again.

The following day, Johnny left, assuring me that he'd be in touch from Texas. I quickly dismantled his makeshift bed, feeling a little heavy-hearted and confused about my feelings for him, once again.

Ripples of heat rose from the busy street when I opened the door for business that day. It was dark with the threat of rain, and there was the rumble of thunder somewhere in the distance. 'I hope Johnny'll be all right,' I said to Violet later on, when she called in.

'Is he coming back?'

'Yes, but I don't know what's going to happen next,' I admitted.

'Just what I thought,' she said, and smiled.

'What is?'

'Are you in love with him?'

'No, you've got it all wrong,' I protested, feeling uncomfortable under her gaze.

'Have I?' she teased.

'Yes, I don't even understand how you could think that. It's not true.' I was angry with her for even suggesting it, but she just laughed at me. 'You think you know me so well, don't you?' I snapped.

'I think I do, Ellie, yes.'

'No, you don't.' I turned and walked off to the back room, Violet's laughter following me. But she didn't come in. A little later I heard the click on the door shutting and she was gone without a goodbye.

In all of the time we'd known each other I'd never had a cross word, and the idea of us falling out upset me, but not as much as her statement that I was in love with Johnny did. Somehow that made me furious.

'You seem very quiet,' Dora said later on.

'Violet and I have had a bit of a tiff,' I admitted.

'Oh?'

'She thinks she knows me so well that she can say what she pleases,' I said, angrily.

'Well, she knows you well enough to speak her mind,' Dora said. 'After all, you've been friends for a long time.'

I looked at her in surprise. 'But what if she's entirely wrong?'

'About what?'

'She says I'm in love with Johnny.'

'And?' Dora looked at me quizzically.

'I'm *not* in love with Johnny,' I said.

'Then you tell her,' she smiled.

So I phoned Violet the next day. 'Hi, Violet. It's me, Ellie.'

'Hi Ellie. Are you all right now?'

'I'm fine, but can we meet?'

'I'll come round later.'

Violet was smiling from ear to ear when she came into the workroom later that afternoon.

'I want you to know that I'm not in love with Johnny,' I told her sternly.

She was silent for a minute. 'Well, perhaps you haven't realised it yet.'

I blushed with annoyance. 'But what about Zak? Don't I love him?'

She sat down. 'Yes, of course you do, Ellie. But maybe you're not *in* love with him.'

'What do you mean, I'm not in love with him?'

'You have a crush on him. You like being with him, and you like the attention he pays you, and why not? He's wonderful, and he treats you as if there's nobody else more important in the world but you when you're together. That doesn't mean you're in love with him. That's something completely different.'

I couldn't take in what she was saying; it didn't make

any sense, because as far as I was concerned I'd been in love with Zak since the first minute I'd set eyes on him.

'I beg to differ—' I started.

Violet sighed. 'Oh, I wish men didn't exist, and then we wouldn't be having this argument. I had to go shopping all on my own yesterday. It's not much fun looking at beautiful clothes and jewellery without you.'

'Why didn't you call for me?'

'I knew I'd upset you and I wanted to give you some time alone to think about what I'd said.'

'Please, Violet, can you stop talking about me and Johnny! There is no me and Johnny. There's me and there's him. Separately.'

Violet laughed. 'Hey, I'm sure you're right.' She held up her hands in surrender.

'I sure am.'

'Right, I won't say another word about it again. By the way, have you heard from him?'

I laughed. 'He called me when he arrived in Texas.'

'What did he say?' She couldn't keep the curiosity out of her voice.

'He just said that he'd arrived safely, and that he was enjoying life on the ranch. Oh, and that he'll be back to see me soon.'

'So your man's coming back to you.'

'Violet, how many times do I have to tell you that he's not my man?'

'I know, but he loves you, Ellie. It is so obvious.

Perhaps he's never stopped loving you.'

'Like a sister maybe. Nothing else!'

'I'm not sure about that. I would give him another chance if I were you. But I'd better stop myself saying anything further, I'm likely to get into more trouble. Anyway, there's only one thing on my mind at the moment.'

'What?'

'The little black dress I saw in Macy's window. I can't stop thinking about it, it's darling.'

'That means you're going to buy it.'

'Well the sales girl is holding it for me, but I'll need your opinion first,' she said, looking at me anxiously.

'Right. Let's go shop!' I said, grabbing my coat.

Twenty-One

'Well, I'll be damned!' said Aunt Mabel when she returned to Boston to hear that Johnny Sheerin had been and gone. 'I've missed him!'

'You knew he was coming over?'

'I suspected it.'

'Why didn't you warn me?'

'I wasn't sure and I knew he'd want it to be a surprise.'

That it certainly had been.

The telephone rang. It was Mr Treacle from the Milliners' Association to tell me that I'd won the Hat Of The Year competition for the most original hat!

'But I didn't enter the competition,' I blustered, in a panic.

'Your store *is* called Chapeau, isn't it?'

'Yes.'

'Crimson-netted smokestack, entered by a Miss Mabel Casey.'

'Aunt Mabel!'

She came rushing out of the kitchen.

'I've won the Hat Of The Year competition!' I

screeched at her, and into poor Mr Treacle's ear. I quickly put down the phone.

'You did! Oh, Ellie! I dreamed about this, and you deserve it. As far as I'm concerned you've done more than your share for the hat trade since you came through Ellis Island.'

'I couldn't have done it without your help, Aunt Mabel.'

'Course you could. If poor Alice hadn't got into difficulties you'd have had your till overflowing with dollar bills.'

Dora, hearing the rumpus, came into the hall. I rushed at her and hugged her as she blinked in confusion. 'We've won the Hat Of The Year competition, Dora . . . For most original hat. This is our prize!'

'It's wonderful news. We're a good team, Ellie, and there's no point in being meek and mild about it. I think we should have a party to celebrate,' she said, grabbing the pen I was holding, starting a list of calls that would have to be made.

'I'm not sure whether it's right to have a party when Alice is in hospital.'

'Alice would be the first to approve,' Aunt Mabel insisted. 'She's not a tragic figure who expects you to put your life on hold until such time as she makes a complete recovery.'

Dora, who loved jazz, perked up. 'We'll have it here.'

'Here!' said Aunt Mabel.

'The place is too small,' I said.

'Open all the doors, put the table out back, and serve cocktails. It'd be good for business,' suggested Dora.

Which was what we did. Dora entered into the spirit of the party with gusto. With her eye for detail and flair for decorating she climbed the stepladder this time to hang bunches of fresh flowers from long ribbons, knotting them here and there. I ran up our frocks, and found a jazz pianist to hire for the evening.

High on success and excitement, we held our party. The place was filled to overflowing. Everyone was most excited, talking and laughing. Aunt Mabel was telling everyone who would listen that from now on I was Boston's star milliner. They all clapped and cheered, and glasses were raised to my success. I let the chatter flow around me, hardly believing my good fortune.

'You've won the hearts of the Boston ladies, and even more importantly the harder hearts of the Milliners' Association,' said an awestruck Mr Samuel.

Everyone arrived. When the party was in full swing, Aunt Mabel asked, 'Who's that guy?' She eyed a latecomer with a smiling face. 'I swear he's the image of Rudolph Valentino,' she said, shaking her head in wonder.

'Zak!' I cried, rushing over to him. Tears stung my eyes at the joy of seeing him again.

'Ellie!' He looked more handsome, more vital than

ever before, as he pushed his hair back from his eyes in that old, familiar gesture.

He lifted me off my feet and whirled me around. His eyes shone with merriment as he said, 'You're a wonder, and you've stolen their hearts.' He was holding me so tightly that I could smell his familiar scent of lemons as he kissed me first on the cheek then full on my lips in front of everyone.

'Put me down,' I squealed, delighted.

I introduced him to Aunt Mabel and, as soon as politeness allowed, we went to sit in a corner of the yard to talk.

'Where did you go?' I asked him.

'I went to stay with my cousin, Mark, in Switzerland first. Had a bit of a holiday with him. It was great doing nothing but sightseeing for a while. Gave me time to think.' He told me all the places he'd been to. I sat there listening to him, finding every word he uttered enthralling.

'What did you think about?' I asked, knowing the answer by the way he was looking at me.

'You.' He told me how he'd planned to travel further when he got the phone call from Violet with the news of Alice's disappearance. 'You should have sent for me, I'd have come back.' As he looked into my eyes I believed him. I'd always been aware of his kindness.

'I'd never have done that,' I said, thinking of all the times I wished he'd been there with me. Oh, I'd been

262

distracted by the 'Gloria thing', as Violet referred to it, from realising just how much he'd done for me since I'd met him, and that made me love him even more. 'I'm glad you're here now.'

'I wanted to see you because I have something important to tell you.'

'What is it?' I was so nervous that my hands were shaking, hoping he wouldn't notice.

'Gloria has gone to England. She's decided to settle down there with a British chap she's been seeing.'

'Never!' My heart almost stopped.

'It's true.' Zak smiled, seeing the expression of shock and disbelief on my face. 'She decided that she preferred the social life over there, so off she went. I thought you'd be pleased to hear it.'

'Well you certainly don't look heartbroken about it.'

He smiled. 'I'm not. I'm pleased for her.' He sounded relieved.

'I hope she'll be very happy,' I said.

'I'm sure she will be. She's a very wealthy lady now that she's come into her inheritance, and she'll have a good time spending it,' he said.

I thought of the bitter things I could say about Gloria and how she'd set her heart on ruining our relationship, instead I said, 'You think I was being silly about her.'

'Not silly, misled, but I can understand that you were insecure,' he said.

That was an understatement, but I let it go, too happy to have Zak back.

'They're playing our tune,' said Zak, pulling me up to dance to 'West End Blues' just as the music stopped.

'Why has the music stopped?' I asked Aunt Mabel. 'I want to dance.'

'It's almost two o'clock in the morning, I think that most of the guests have gone.'

I hadn't even noticed.

'I'd better go too,' Zak said. 'I'll call in to see you tomorrow.' He took my hand, gave me a respectful kiss on the cheek, said goodnight to Aunt Mabel and went, leaving me trembling from head to toe.

Next day, when I got back from the deli with our lunch, Zak and Aunt Mabel were sitting together at the kitchen table, Zak laughing at something she'd said, his head inclined towards her. I stood at the door, taking in the scene before me. He saw me, got to his feet. 'Ellie! Your aunt has been entertaining me with stories about her time in New York when she was young,' he said.

'Really!' I said, blushing like a schoolgirl.

'I just dropped by to see how you were.'

'Won't you stay for a bite to eat?' Aunt Mabel asked him.

Zak looked questioningly at me, a light of amusement in his eyes.

'We'd love to have you.'

264

Over lunch he paid Aunt Mabel a great deal of attention as she regaled him with stories of her past. Dora went back to work; Aunt Mabel excused herself, and said that she was going to have a lie down.

Zak came and sat down beside me. 'Would you like to have dinner with me tomorrow evening?'

'I'd love to.'

When he left, Aunt Mabel came downstairs. 'He's a most handsome young man, and judging by how well-dressed he is he's got plenty of money.' She peered at me from behind her spectacles. 'Imagine if he married you.'

'Don't be silly,' I laughed.

She raised her eyes to me. 'It's not a silly idea, and think of the possibilities. You'd never be in want, Ellie.' She looked at me seriously.

'Oh, I'm not so sure.' I told her all about his parents' disapproval of me, and about their wish for him to marry Gloria. 'I thought that I was never going to be the one for him, Aunt Mabel.'

'Rubbish! I knew the moment he walked in. I said to myself – he's perfect for Ellie. A blind man on a galloping horse could see how happy he is with you.'

'I'm not sure.' I bit my lip.

'Well. There's no point in hanging on to him if you're not certain that he's the one you love, the one that you can't live without.'

'Oh, Aunt Mabel, you're such a romantic,' I laughed.

She shook her head. 'What I'm saying is true. Unless

you want to spend the rest of your life with him it's no good. Believe me, I know. I was always doubtful about my fiancé, Chandler, and I was proved right. You know for a long time I used to picture him on board ship, windswept and looking out to sea, pining for me. But obviously he didn't miss me enough to want to marry me, because all of our plans came to nothing, and, to tell the truth, I didn't pine for him for very long either.'

That afternoon a reporter from the *Boston Globe* phoned.

Aunt Mabel said, 'You've got to go talk to someone at the *Boston Globe*, Ellie.'

Zak phoned immediately afterwards. 'Have you forgotten about our dinner date?' He sounded disappointed.

'The press are waiting for me to give an interview,' I said, practically rushing out the door. 'Give me an hour. As soon as I've changed out of these clothes I'll come back.'

'Don't take too long, I can't wait to see you.'

I was shaking with nerves, hoping the reporter wouldn't notice, as I told him the whole story of my hat business. I told him about Aunt Mabel coming to the rescue when things got bad. 'I'm going to miss her so much when she leaves.' He was very interested in the fact that Eamon was still at large, writing it all down.

Zak was waiting for me in the restaurant, the newspaper spread out in front of him. 'Well, I see you're becoming famous.'

'And what's wrong with that?' I laughed, high on the success of the interview.

'Oh, I'm not going to try and persuade you against it – quite the opposite. Your hats are going to be big in the future. In fact there isn't a ladies' rendezvous where they're not being discussed, I hear. By the way, there's a larger store up for rent a block away. I think you're going to need it.'

After our meal he took me to see the new store at the end of Charles Street. The windows and door were blocked, dandelions sprouted unchecked from the walls. Inside was clean and empty. From upstairs we looked down on row after row of rooftops, with the church spire at the end.

'This is a terrible place,' I said in disgust.

'It's the right location though. There's a new clothes store opening up on the corner. If you open early and close late you'll get their business.'

'I'm not sure.'

'If you don't make up your mind there's a good chance it'll be gone. It's an executor sale; it's in a primary location. This is a good shopping street. You're perfectly placed among the best stores.'

True enough, the other stores were painted bright

colours; flags snapped from their windows.

'I'll never fill this place with hats,' I said, walking around.

'Buy in bulk, it's cheaper, and you'll only need to order once a month or so.'

'I could never afford it.'

'You could if you took on a proper partner.'

'I wouldn't want to share my business with anyone—'

'—one who would be willing to help out if necessary.'

I looked at him. 'You mean you'd be interested in a share of my business.'

'I think it'd be a great investment. You're going places, lady, and I'm coming with you – that's if you'll have me,' he said shyly.

I thought for just a second. 'I think I'll paint it pink – fuchsia-pink. What do you think?'

Aunt Mabel left for Brooklyn, without any fuss at all. This time she was going for good, taking Alice back to Ireland with her.

Before she climbed into the back of the waiting cab, she opened her handbag and took out an envelope. 'This is a little something to keep you going until you're on your feet again.'

'Oh, Aunt Mabel, I can't take it, you've done enough for me already.'

'Course you can,' she said, hugging me. 'Keep going,

you're doing wonderfully well. And don't worry about Alice, I'll take very good care of her. She'll be fine.'

I didn't want her to go. I wanted to throw myself into her arms to stop her from leaving, but instead I smiled and waved her off, my throat in a tight knot of sadness.

'Well!' said Dora. 'I see what you mean about her. She's one powerful lady.'

Epilogue

From my top floor workroom I watch the leaves in the park change to crimson, burnt orange, russet and gold. I could never have dreamed of having such a magnificent view, and such a spacious room. Dora has a whole corner to herself. This is where we plan our working day and talk about all manner of things concerning our business, as she is now a junior partner.

I named the store Chapeau Chapeau, on account of all the extra hats we have on sale. I love to see clients stop in their tracks, surprised by the vastness of it. In the window there is a sample of each divine hat, while I keep drawings of variations of them on the counter for our clients to choose from. This season I have made a more youthful line of hats. We sell them faster than we can make them, and we make them fast. We're there all of the time, working night and day. They are becoming a household name.

Mr Samuel walked into Chapeau Chapeau one morning soon after we opened. His eyes lit up when he saw the amount of space we had. 'Big enough to sell my sportswear,' he said, cool as could be, looking around with his measuring eyes.

'It's a hat shop, Sammy. I don't think sportswear belongs here,' I told him.

'I won't argue with you, but at least think about it, Ellie. I'll make it worth your while . . . If you change your mind, let me know. Remember I was the one who recognised that sportswear was going to boom, and I was right. And your shares are doing well from it.'

That was true. My shares in his business were rising, and I was increasingly busy designing new outfits for it. But I still resisted the temptation to display the garments, fearing that my clients might be distracted from their point of purchase.

When his persuasive charms failed, he sent Shirlee in to try and coax me round to his way of thinking.

'I don't know why he needs an outlet. His business is booming, so much so that I never see him,' Shirlee complained when she came to admire the new store. 'When he's home he needs to rush off to the factory. When he's at the factory he's trying to get away to play golf, or have dinner with a client. He's always in a hurry.'

'I think it's a great idea. Give him the upstairs,' said the resourceful Zak as we were walking home from the cinema one evening.

'And where will I live?'

'What about my apartment? There's room enough for two.'

'Oh Zak! I couldn't live with you. People would talk,' I protested.

'That's what I've been meaning to ask you, Ellie. Will you marry me?'

'What did you say?' It was the last thing I'd expected to hear. I wondered if he'd been carried away by the movie we'd just seen, *The Phantom Of The Opera*.

'I asked you to marry me.'

'But I can't. Your parents made it clear that they didn't think I was good enough for their son last time you offered to marry me.'

'My folks' opinion doesn't count, Ellie, and they know it,' he said, reading my mind. 'What matters is you and me, and it's all different now. I'm desperately in love with you, Ellie.' He took me in his arms and kissed me.

Dizzily, I looked up at him.

'Ellie!' he groaned, kissing me again. This time it was a fierce passionate kiss that made my heart beat wildly. All I could do was gaze up into his eyes, spellbound.

'I'd love to marry you,' I told him when we broke apart.

Side by side, we sat on a park bench for a long time making our future plans while watching people pass down the sidewalk on their way home. We watched the sun set, trailing an orange glow across the sky. Zak put his arm around me and pulled me close as we strolled home, through the rustling leaves that had been blown down in the wind.

All of the family attended our wedding, except for Uncle Jack and Aunt Sally. It would have been too embarrassing for them to come now that Eamon is safely behind bars. They blame Alice for that, but as Zak says, you cannot virtually kidnap someone and expect to get away with it.

Aunt Mabel created me a wedding dress with long train and a veil that flowed from a crown of roses. She stayed on after the wedding to help me out in the store, but mainly to be with Arnie Walker. He's sweet on her, and she on him, so much so that she's thinking of selling her hat shop in Ireland and coming to live here for good.

Johnny came all the way from Texas to attend the wedding. He was his old self, broad-shouldered and handsome as ever. He's bought a bit of land and is herding his own cattle now. He spent most of the time with Violet. She's sweet on him, and he seems to like her a lot too. I wouldn't be surprised if they end up together, judging by the way they were mooning over one another. Wouldn't it be a hoot if my best friend were to marry my childhood sweetheart?

Alice is here with us too. She refused to stay in Ireland because she still wants to go to college. She is blossoming into a beautiful girl. She's taller, her limbs are smooth, her walk more graceful than ever. She is happier too, racing off to meet her friends, her hair a mass of curls piled up on her head, her eyes bright, her smile mischievous, just like before her illness. She's attending the local school, and with each day she is growing closer to me again; the nightmare of Eamon is all but forgotton.

Bridget came to the wedding. She too stayed on to look after Alice while we honeymooned in Paris, and she never returned to Brooklyn. She is a tower of strength to us all, and we adore her.

PS
When I left Ireland, I moved away from everything I'd known, and there was a gaping hole in my life. This had left me always longing for something. Now, everything I want is here with me in America, and I am happy.
Love,
Ellie

Eleanor Rubens 1926

Read the beginning of Ellie's adventure in:

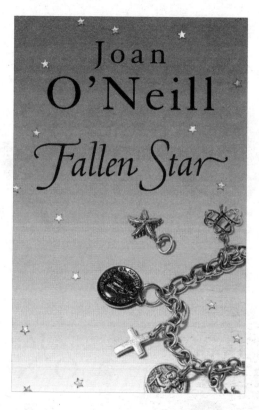

In Ireland, in 1959, fifteen year old Stella is growing up in the small coastal town of Knocknacree, spending her Saturdays working at the seafront café, daydreaming about a better future. Then charismatic young Charles Thornton walks into the café and sweeps Stella off her feet. Giddy with happiness, Stella is having fun – and taking risks. Nothing could possibly spoil her happiness now … could it?

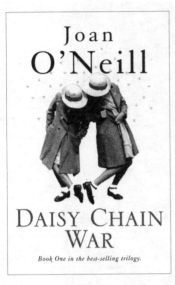

Joan
O'Neill

DAISY CHAIN
WAR

Book One in the best-selling trilogy.

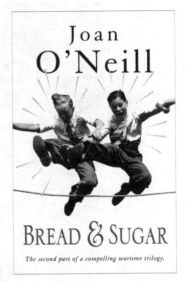

Joan
O'Neill

BREAD & SUGAR

The second part of a compelling wartime trilogy.

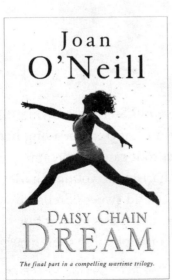

Joan
O'Neill

DAISY CHAIN
DREAM

The final part in a compelling wartime trilogy.

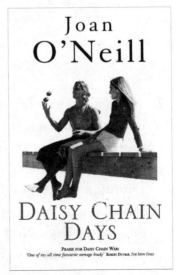

Joan
O'Neill

DAISY CHAIN
DAYS

PRAISE FOR DAISY CHAIN WAR:
'One of my all time favourite teenage books' ROBERT DUNBAR, *The Irish Times*